THE
LAST
LINE
OF THEIR
LIVES

a novel

ANDREW D. DOAN

Copyright © 2021 by Andrew D. Doan

All rights reserved.

This novel is entirely a work of fiction. The names, characters and incidents portrayed in it are the work of the author's imagination. Any resemblance to actual persons, living or dead, events or localities is entirely coincidental.

No part of this book may be reproduced in any form or by any electronic or mechanical means, including information storage and retrieval systems, without written permission from the author, except for the use of brief quotations in a book review.

Scripture quotation taken from the *King James Version*

Cover Design by Jenneth Dyck

Paperback ISBN 978-1-7375610-0-2
Ebook ISBN 978-1-7375610-1-9

To Paul
Next time lunch is on me.

And on the pedestal these words appear:
   "My name is Ozymandias, king of kings:
   Look on my works, ye Mighty, and despair!"

Nothing beside remains. Round the decay
   Of that colossal wreck, boundless and bare
   The lone and level sands stretch far away.

— FROM "OZYMANDIAS" BY PERCY BYSSHE SHELLEY

CHAPTER 1

To Dr. Greg Patterson, dying was no big deal. Though he had yet to die himself, his career of more than three decades had brought him face to face with death hundreds of times. Rarely had he flinched. Since his earliest days in medical school, he'd been able to strip mortality of its vestments and see its naked biology at work—thorough and mercilessly efficient.

On a Monday evening in early fall, Dr. Greg drove from his private practice on the southwest side of Emmitsville, Pennsylvania, to Harold Tomlinson's home. Though Greg had assured the family that the hospice nurse was fully capable of handling the situation, Harold's wife and sons had been insisting on regular visits from an M.D. for over a month.

"He hasn't spoken since yesterday afternoon." It was Harold's oldest son, Dan. "I don't think he's opened his eyes today at all. The nurse left around lunchtime, and we've been letting him rest since then."

"OK, Dan. I'll take a look."

Greg stepped into Harold's bedroom and closed the door. "Hello, Harold."

The old man was slumped on his side, facing the wall. As soon as Greg walked around the end of the bed and saw

Harold's face, he knew the man was dead. After confirming this, Greg rested two of his fingers lightly on Harold's forehead. Then he returned to the living room where Dan was waiting.

Three days later Greg sat near the back of the Robert C. Hunt Memorial Chapel—the bright, spacious crown jewel of the Cotterman Funeral Home and Memorial Gardens.

"Good morning, Doc!" An old man in a dark pinstripe suit was hobbling up the aisle. Greg waved back. "Hello, Artis."

"Think old Howard will fill up the overflow rooms today?"

"It's early yet, Artis."

With its vaulted ceiling and wide padded chairs, the chapel could hold just under 500 people. Two overflow rooms with closed-circuit projection screens accommodated another 150 mourners each. Only two funerals that had ever taken place there had filled all three rooms to capacity, though several had come close. People in town often talked about who among them would be next to accomplish this feat.

Ambrose and Allen Wannamaker, the funeral home's co-operators, stood at the chapel entrance and greeted their guests. Although Greg's relationship with the brothers was based primarily on the close connection between his work as town physician and theirs as funeral directors, he considered them his friends. Maybe not close friends, but good acquaintances.

Like Artis, nearly every person who walked through the double doors at the end of the center aisle was a patient of Dr. Greg. As one of only a few full-time physicians in the valley, his business was booming—and not just because of his near monopoly in the area. In Emmitsville, the average age was fifty-seven, the life expectancy seventy-nine, and the median income well past the six-digit barrier.

As the stream of finely clothed men and women entering

the room slowed to a trickle, it was obvious that Harold's funeral would fall well short of the acclaimed benchmark.

At exactly eleven o'clock, a door at the front of the chapel opened and eight young men in tailed tuxedos entered with silver serving platters perched on their fingers. They began moving among the funeral attendees like the wait staff at a state dinner while the crowd stared in intrigued silence. Instead of hors d'oeuvres, the men handed each attendee a cigar and a stainless-steel lighter engraved with the letters *HOT*.

Then another tuxedoed man—older than the cigar butlers —entered and stood on the stage, above the dozens of flower arrangements. He held up a wireless microphone.

"Ladies and gentlemen! Welcome to the main event!"

A rhythmic beat began to pound from the speakers.

"Are you ready to rumble?"

He held out the word *rumble* for a few seconds as the music grew louder. The crowd remained silent. Unflappable, the emcee pressed on.

"And now . . . let's welcome the man of the hour—the one, the only, Harold . . . Orson . . . Tomlinson!"

Cheering and thunderous applause bounced around the room. Greg leaned forward to see where the noise was coming from. Everyone that he could see was sitting and staring. Greg realized that the crowd sounds were part of the music track.

The entrance doors swung open and Harold's two sons wheeled in the casket, followed by Harold's wife, daughter, grandchildren, and several people Greg didn't recognize. The shimmering black casket had a gold inlay engraved with an intricate, Celtic-looking design. Its sleek, rounded corners and edges gave the whole container the look of a dapper sports car.

After Harold had been rolled gently to a stop at the front

of the chapel and the processional had been seated on the first row, Dan approached the wooden podium onstage.

"Good morning, everyone. Thank you for being here today. I speak for all of my family—and for my dad—when I say that it means a lot to us that you came out for this service.

"Dad loved sports of all kinds. Football. Basketball. Racing. Golf. He especially loved boxing. It was always one of his favorites. He did a little of it back during his days in the army. He loved going to watch a good bout . . . or two . . . or three! He was able to see some pretty big fights, too! Bowe versus Holyfield, Tyson versus Spinks—he was a little disappointed at how short that one was since he'd paid for an entire skybox of seats! He even got to see Ali fight once. Oh, yes! He loved being there in the middle of it all. He always dreamed about being in the spotlight—about being welcomed into the ring like a champion."

Dan looked up tenderly. "Well, Dad. You're finally getting your chance. Your big introduction. You're ready to rumble and so are we."

Greg looked up as well. Staring at the ceiling, he thought, *You watching all this, Harold? Maybe you're a little busy just now.*

"Anyway, we're really glad you're all here," Dan continued. "What a crowd! Dad was a powerful man. He built his life and his fortune from the ground up, and he deserves to have so many people hear about his spectacular life. A great crowd for a great man! Thank you."

A prayer and Scripture reading followed. Then the lights dimmed, and a large screen unraveled from the ceiling. Classic rock songs blared as a montage of photos scrolled across the screen.

The images told the story of a boy who was born in the Great Depression, came of age during the post–World War II boom, and established his niche in the world of industrial manufacturing in the early 60's. It became obvious to anyone who didn't already know the story that Harold hit pay dirt shortly after. His clothes became newer and finer. The houses and landscapes behind him grew larger and more opulent. Golf courses. Court-side seats. Snowbound chalets on remote mountainsides. Harold's smile looked as if it expanded over the years as well—often punctuated by a cigar on one side.

After the slide show, the eulogies began. Harold's other son, his best friend, and a woman named Doreen extolled his virtues, though Greg felt—as he often did when listening to funeral orations—that the sentiments were trite, generalized, and likely exaggerated.

The final segment of the service featured Eric Pettigrew, senior manager at the Emmitsville branch of the Pennsylvania First Trust Bank. He timidly read an announcement that his branch would henceforth be known as the Harold O. Tomlinson Branch of the Pennsylvania First Trust Bank. The bank's board was giving Harold this honor in return for his many years of patronage and support. A pewter plaque near the bank's front entrance would announce to all who entered the board's gratitude for Harold.

The recessional began. Leaving the casket at the front, Harold's loved ones trudged slowly back down the aisle as a recording of the 60's ballad "The Boxer" played in the background.

Greg watched his patients and neighbors empty out of the chapel as he fiddled with the silver lighter in his hand. Never one to enjoy crowds or small talk, he waited until the room was nearly cleared before leaving.

"What a lovely service!" Jane Lerner, in her late seventies and a longtime resident of Emmitsville, was shaking hands with Ambrose Wannamaker near the chapel entrance. "Dignified and smooth as always."

"Thank you, ma'am." Ambrose wore a deep-green tie and a black suit that seemed slightly too spacious for his long torso. "You know we always aim for excellence."

"You do, indeed." Jane patted his hand. "And you always

hit your mark, as far as I'm concerned. Cotterman funerals are simply the best. Everyone in town knows it."

"I hope that's true."

"It's just a shame the cemetery isn't bigger. I've always felt the property could've been planned better. Wouldn't you agree?"

"Um . . ." Ambrose spotted Greg scooting past them. "Perhaps—would you excuse me?"

"Certainly."

"Greg! Can you hold on a moment?"

Greg paused by the front door. "Nice service today. A little odd, but memorable."

"Yes." Ambrose looked around the lobby for any lingering guests before loosening his tie and top shirt button. The lines on his face were deep from years of solemnly tending to the final arrangements of Emmitsville's departed.

"I think the bank thing is kinda funny." Greg commented.

"What do you mean?"

"Well, it's a branch of a midlevel regional bank. Not terribly prestigious. Do you really think that's how Harold wanted to be remembered for all time?"

"Perhaps not, but he will be remembered, won't he?"

"At least until they tear the building down."

"I appreciate your cynical wit, but I need to ask you a serious favor."

A pair of stragglers emerged from the chapel—two old men engaged in a heated discussion about Muhammad Ali and George Foreman as they hobbled through the lobby.

Ambrose cinched up his tie without refastening the button. "Maybe it would be better for me to explain when we have more time and privacy. Allen and I have to get the casket loaded into the hearse. The graveside service begins soon at Bluebird Meadows."

"No pallbearers?"

"Harold didn't name any."

"Didn't want the hassle of narrowing down a list and ticking off anyone who didn't make the cut."

Ambrose ignored the comment. "Could I come by your office tomorrow morning?"

"Sure. I've got a few patients to see early, but around ten thirty would work."

"Perfect. Thanks. See you then." Ambrose turned toward the chapel.

"You said a serious favor? Just how serious are we talking here?"

"*Advice* is probably a better way to put it. I need some advice."

"Serious advice?" Ambrose nodded. "How serious?"

"That depends, of course, but it could be quite so."

"Now you got me curious."

"I'll tell you all about it in the morning."

Ambrose rushed to meet his brother, who was waiting by Harold's casket. Greg walked to his car, still holding the lighter an old man had given him from the grave.

CHAPTER 2

*C*offee mug in hand, Greg sat on a wooden bench not far from the front door of his office and watched customers walk in and out of the deli across the street.

Greg housed his practice in a narrow brick building that had once been a shoe shop. It was in a row of single-story storefronts on the north end of Second Street, one of the four main roads running the length of Emmitsville. A dozen other brick buildings like his squatted shoulder to shoulder along the road. Like most of the town, this street was clean and well-groomed but lacked the updated elegance one might expect from a place where most residents were wealthy.

Fifteen years earlier, Greg had pulled a moving trailer into town after the half-day drive south from Boston. The first thing he did after finding an apartment was set up his practice. As Greg became acquainted with his new patients, he realized many of their stories were nearly identical.

"Oh, yes! My family had a summer home here when I was growing up."

"My parents moved here after the war. I went to boarding school in Connecticut while they lived in Emmitsville."

"I can remember when this place was bustling with celebrities and politicians nearly every weekend!"

"When it was time to retire, we both knew there was no other place for us but here."

It was the bit about retiring there that puzzled Greg.

Originally founded in the late 1800s as the town of Washington's Corner, Emmitsville hadn't started out as a luxurious hub for the well-to-do. The earliest residents were loggers and their families. The town's rags began turning to riches around 1906 with the arrival of Emmit S. Willingham, owner of the region's largest logging corporation. As Emmit's wealth had grown over the years, he'd decided he wanted a hillside retreat to call his own. Washington's Corner, in the shadow of the Poconos and just a day's journey from New York City, was precisely what he was looking for.

Emmit Willingham was a powerful and charismatic person. His money and influence transformed tiny, timid Washington's Corner into Emmitsville, a lavish retreat for the rich, by the 1920s.

But though the town had been opulent and glistening half a century ago, much of its glory had since faded away. The money that built Emmitsville was old, rooted in the industries of the Progressive Era and the Roaring Twenties. Many of the town's most successful tycoons declined to adapt to the new technologies of the twentieth century. They preferred to cash in, check out, and pass their wealth on to their descendants.

The generation that remained when Greg rolled into town was trying to keep the posh party going that their parents and grandparents had begun. But it was obvious (to Greg at least) that the luster just wasn't there.

Greg drained the last drops from his mug and rose from the bench. He pulled open the glass door leading into his waiting room just in time to hear his receptionist, Gladys, speak with an air of suspicion.

"Well, Betty, I'm pretty sure she was more than just an assistant. Wouldn't you say?"

Betty ran a dry-cleaning service two doors down and often popped over for tea and gossip with Gladys.

"You really think so? Gosh! I can't even imagine how that must've made Mindy feel. She and Harold were married for so long."

"There's a difference between being married and being happily married."

"I guess you're right." Betty started to sip her tea, then stopped short. "But wait! If Mindy knew Harold was horsin' around with—what's her name?"

"Doreen."

"If Mindy knew Harold was horsin' around with Doreen, she never would've stayed. She's too feisty to put up with that nonsense."

Gladys lowered her reading glasses on her nose and leaned toward Betty with a mischievous smile. "You're right. Mindy would never stay *if* she knew Harold was cheating. Obviously, she didn't know."

"Obviously." Greg plopped into one of the waiting-room chairs. "Or maybe—and I'm just taking a stab in the dark— maybe Harold wasn't cheating at all?"

Gladys retorted, "Then how do you explain the fact that Doreen spoke at the service when Mindy did not?"

"Stage fright?"

Unimpressed, Gladys crossed her arms. "You're hilarious."

"Who said I was joking?" Greg thumbed through one of the outdated magazines Gladys kept around for waiting patients.

"Either way it just seems odd to me that this mysterious woman gave such an emotional and personal eulogy for someone she wasn't even married to."

"If that's the only thing about the funeral that struck you as odd, then maybe you and I have less in common than I thought." He said it with a smile, and Gladys rolled her eyes in playful indignation.

"You didn't like the funeral, Doctor?" Betty turned toward Greg from where she stood by Gladys's desk.

"He doesn't like any funerals. Isn't that right, Doctor?" Greg shrugged.

Betty watched Greg with an infatuated expression that would have embarrassed her if she had seen it. "Really? I never knew that about you. What will you do when you—you know, when you . . ." She let her voice trail off.

"When I die?"

Betty nodded. Greg continued flipping magazine pages.

"I'll probably take his ashes out to some godforsaken hiking trail in the middle of Podunk, Pennsylvania, and toss him to the wind!"

"You two crack me up!" Betty held her teacup tightly in both hands. "But, seriously, don't you think your family will want some sort of service? Or maybe your wife?"

Greg stared at the glossy pages in his hands and tried not to feel self-conscious. Gladys's words from moments earlier seemed apropos. *There's a difference between being married and being happily married.*

"You know? I'm not exactly sure what the Patterson clan will do when my time comes around." He tossed the magazine onto the coffee table and shrugged again. "I guess I should get that all figured out soon, huh?"

The door opened. "Ah! Ambrose! You're just in time."

Ambrose Wannamaker stared in confusion. "I try never to be late."

"I meant, you're just in time to rescue me from—from . . ."

Gladys pounced. "From what, Doctor?"

"Embarrassing myself?"

"Hmm . . . no comment."

Greg motioned down the hallway that led past the

reception desk to his private office. "Shall we?" Ambrose nodded.

In the office, Greg leaned on the edge of his desk and studied Ambrose, who sat on a cream-colored chair, tapping his foot in an irregular, rapid rhythm.

"What's going on, Ambrose?"

"It's about the cemetery—about Cotterman." Ambrose looked at the floor and smoothed his pants with his hands.

"What about it?"

"Well, it looks like we're going to have some extra space, and I don't know what to do about it."

"Space for what?"

"Customers."

"Customers. You mean . . . like . . . dead people?"

"Yes."

Greg leaned forward and grinned. "Did some grave robbers come through and empty out a few caskets?"

"I'm coming here for help, Greg. I know you like to tease me, but I really don't feel this is the time for it. This situation was plopped into our lap out of the blue and could get out of hand very quickly!" His foot continued to pound the carpet beneath him.

Greg slid from his perch on the desk into the other guest chair. "OK. I'm sorry. Obviously this has you upset, and I shouldn't be making light of it."

"Thank you."

Greg's conciliatory approach soothed Ambrose, and his posture loosened as his foot finally came to rest.

"Tell me about this extra space. I mean, ordinarily it would be a good thing, right?"

"Ordinarily, yes, but the problem is figuring out who to sell these extra spots to."

"Just sell 'em to whoever wants 'em." Greg waved a hand dismissively.

"That's the problem. I've suddenly got six burial plots, but

I'm quite certain that many more than that will want to buy them."

"Is there a gold mine beneath them or something?"

"Not quite. You know about the history of Cotterman, don't you?"

"A little, I guess. It's the oldest cemetery in town and it's considered the best one around by most people, though I've never really understood how one cemetery can be any better or worse than another. Everyone in them is equally dead, right?"

"Setting aside that there can be huge differences from one cemetery to another—just take Woodland Acres, for example."

"Over on Route 402?"

Ambrose rolled his eyes. "Yes. Don't get me started on those folks over there. So, setting that obvious fact aside, the real problem for us is that it's not just *any* cemetery we're talking about. It's Cotterman."

"You really think it's that big of a deal?"

"What I think is irrelevant, though the funeral home and burial ground are obviously quite important to me because of my family history there."

"Of course."

"It's what the people around town think. That's what matters." Ambrose stared through the office window as though he could see past the adjacent building and take in a view of the entire valley. "To most of them, Cotterman is as important to the town as City Hall or their own homes."

"Not gonna lie to you. That's downright baffling to me." Greg walked to the wall behind them and retrieved a few darts from an old-fashioned dart board hanging near the door. He lined up next to his desk and took aim.

"As I said before, it's all about the history of the cemetery itself."

Greg let the first dart fly. It sank deep into the corkboard with a *thwump* just shy of the bull's-eye. "So what is it?"

"It's Mr. Willingham—Emmit Willingham. He established Cotterman in 1915 after his oldest son, Robert, died when the *Lusitania* sank at the start of World War I."

"Oh yeah!" Greg squinted and tried to zero in on the center of the board. "I've heard that part before."

"When Emmit heard the news, he planned for Robert to be buried on the Willingham estate in England. Somehow that was never properly communicated, and three weeks later Emmit received a telegram that his son's remains were waiting at the port at Baltimore . . . Maryland."

"That's some substantial miscommunication."

"Sadly, not as rare as you might think. You'd be surprised how often bodies are shipped to the wrong location or lost in the system altogether. It's an unfortunate downside in the industry.

"When Robert's body was delivered here in town it was— well, let me put it this way—it was painfully obvious that they needed to conduct a burial as quickly as possible."

Greg had seen many corpses, but few of them had been decomposing at the time. "I can imagine."

"So Emmit made a quick decision. He cleared a spot of land on his property west of town and laid Robert's remains to rest within just a few days. That would have been the end of it if someone hadn't approached him with an idea—why not clear more land and create a new town cemetery? Emmitsville was growing, so there was need for a bigger one.

"I'm not sure how much you know about Emmit Willingham, Greg, but he was shrewd, particularly in business, and he was charismatic. He had a way of influencing people that was powerful."

Greg had thrown all his darts. He sat down in the chair behind his desk. "I've heard bits and pieces. Did you ever meet him?"

"Oh, heavens! No! He passed away long before I was born. But my father told me about him many times. Father worked for Mr. Willingham most of his life.

"Emmit saw an opportunity to make money with the burial ground. He put out an order to clear more land—several acres—and immediately began advertising that burial plots were for sale. It set off a frenzy around town. As my father tells it, folks were practically throwing money at Emmit in order to get a spot."

"That makes no sense to me."

"It's not that difficult to imagine. Don't forget that many of the townsfolk around at that time were the same people that approved Emmit's ballot measure to rename the town after himself. They adored him—practically worshipped the man. My father always found that curious.

"If Emmit Willingham was creating a cemetery and offering his neighbors a chance to own part of it, then there were more than enough people willing to pay top dollar for the privilege. All the land was sold and reserved within months. Most of the land went to twenty or so of the richest men in town. They purchased whole sections of the cemetery for themselves and their families. Individual buyers gobbled up whatever spots were left over."

"So he was all out of room right from the get-go."

"Only in a manner of speaking. All of the burial plots were reserved, but his son Robert was the only one actually buried there at the time. After the selling frenzy was over, it simply became a matter of gradually filling up the cemetery as the plot owners and their family members passed away over the years."

"OK . . . so how do we go from that to six open slots a hundred years later?"

"If you ask most people around here, they'll tell you that Cotterman has been full for a while. That's not technically true. It's been *nearly* full ever since we buried John Wagner."

Greg perked up. "Hey! I remember him. He died shortly after I got here. He was one of the patients I inherited from Dr. Amsbaugh's practice. Bone cancer, as I recall."

"Yes. Though we haven't had a Cotterman burial since then, technically there's been a sliver of land open near the eastern edge of the cemetery."

"Belonging to . . . ?"

"The Cohen family."

"Never heard of them."

"Jacob Cohen made his fortune in garment sales. I met him once when I was a kid. A very pleasant man. He was one of those original twenty who grabbed as many spots as he could for his children and grandchildren. He divided up the family plot among his three boys and their families.

"David, his youngest, and David's wife Marie never had any children. Both of them are buried in Cotterman, but the six plots meant for their family are still open. When David died, his portion of the land reverted back to the family estate, but no one in the extended Cohen clan has ever claimed any of the spots.

"My guess is that they don't find it as important as the older generations in the family. Even David and Marie seemed ambivalent about the whole thing. I'm pretty sure they only used their part of the land because it was already paid for.

"So fast-forward to yesterday morning when we received a letter from the Cohens' lawyer informing us that the family estate is officially revoking their claim on the land and returning it to the cemetery. They didn't even ask for a refund on their money. I'm not sure who made the decision, but it's obvious they have no interest in fulfilling their great-great-grandfather's wishes."

Greg stretched his arms toward the ceiling and took in a giant breath. "OK. So now I'm up to speed. You've got six burial plots, and you're fairly sure there could be another buying frenzy over them."

"Not 'fairly sure.' I'm certain of it. There's a good number of people in town who know about the Cohen plot. They've been in Emmitsville long enough to know the story. I get asked about it every so often—Allen, too."

"What do you tell people when they ask?"

"I tell them that I'm sure the Cohen family will use their spots eventually—because that's what I believed until yesterday."

"Yeah, but knowing about the land and buying it aren't the same thing. Maybe the people asking are just curious bystanders."

Ambrose shook his head firmly. "No. That's not true. They're asking because they want the spots for themselves. I'm sure of it. Do you know the woman who was chatting with me after Harold's service? Right before I spoke with you?"

"Jane Lerner. Sure. I know her."

"Jane attends every funeral we hold regardless of whether she has any connection to the deceased. She sits through the service and then makes it a point to find me afterward and tell me how wonderful of a job we've done once again. It's always the same. Cotterman is such a beautiful place. We do such a fine job. It's just a shame there's not more room out there."

Ambrose slumped back in his chair, glum and anxious.

"So this is the part where you want my advice, is that right?"

"There's really no one else in town I'd bring this to. In all the years I've known you, you've seemed to be a logical, straightforward thinker and a problem solver. Allen and I figured you'd be able to look at our situation clearly without all the history and sentimentality clouding your vision."

"You don't think I'm sentimental?" Greg feigned surprise.

"Not particularly."

"OK then. Let me put my unsentimental powers of logic to work here." Greg went to the dart board and pulled out the darts, then set himself in line with it again. "You know? It kind of reminds me of Oklahoma."

"Pardon me?"

"The Oklahoma Land Rush. They had some land. People wanted the land. So they let everyone know that on such and such date at such and such time the land was up for grabs. First come, first served."

"You're suggesting we conduct a land rush?"

"It's unconventional, but if the interest in your cemetery is as high as you say, you shouldn't have a problem selling all six spots right away. Then your problem disappears. Cotterman will be completely, officially, unarguably full!" He launched a dart with a sharp snap of his wrist.

"But what about those who get left out?"

"They figure something else out. Woodland Acres, Bluebird Meadows, cremation, cryogenics. There's plenty of options."

"But only one Cotterman. That's what they'll say."

"They're right about that. There's only one Cotterman, and they won't get a spot in it. They'll just have to deal with the loss."

"You've been around here long enough to know that many of our mutual clientele are unaccustomed to not getting what they want."

"That's for sure. But what else can you do?"

Ambrose took out the darts one by one from the board. "How would we conduct this 'land rush'? How would we determine who claims the spots first? Do we ask people to come to the funeral home? Call? Send a letter? What if Allen and I come to work on that day to find fifty people waiting outside our door? What then?"

"You could auction them off. Highest bidder?"

"You mean like an actual auction? Live?"

"Sure. You could host it at the funeral home."

"I don't know. Something about all of this feels very . . ." Ambrose bit his lower lip until he settled on a word. "Cheap."

"I'd expect the auction bids to be quite high."

"That's not what I mean. It feels . . . profane, somehow. I can't picture my father ever doing something like this."

"Your father's not here, Ambrose. You are. It's your cemetery. You've got to decide." Greg cocked his arm to fling another dart, but stopped short and held it aloft. "You know! Another possibility just occurred to me."

"Something better, I hope!"

"Maybe the land rush isn't to see who buys the burial plots first, but who actually needs them first. Anybody who's interested can throw their name in the hat, so to speak, and from that group the first six people to die get the spots. See? It gives everyone an equal chance, and it leaves the task of deciding to . . . whoever or whatever!"

"You're suggesting a waiting list?"

"Basically, yes." Greg tried to read Ambrose's furrowed features. "Still too profane?"

"Not necessarily. It's odd, but it could work."

"I'm sure it would work. Eventually, six people around here will die—and when they do, you can finally fill up Emmit Willingham's cemetery."

"I'll need to talk it over with my brother, of course."

"In the meantime, my best advice is to keep all of this quiet. You said that most everyone assumes Cotterman is full. You might as well let them go on thinking that until you and Allen figure out what you want to do."

Ambrose left, and Greg retrieved the darts once more. As he threw them at the board, he mulled over the conversation, trying to decide if Ambrose was overreacting.

Through fifteen years of practice in Emmitsville, he'd come to recognize the town's eccentricity, so it wasn't farfetched to imagine the six spots in Cotterman causing a stir. Yet he found it difficult to picture the frenzy that Ambrose feared.

"Who knows?"

He let the last dart loose. His fingers fudged as he released it, sending the dart far to the right of the board, where it sank into the wall below Greg's med-school diploma.

CHAPTER 3

wo weeks later, Darren Horowitz, a sixty-two-year-old silver-spoon son of a steel magnate, threw a tennis ball into the air as he prepared to serve to his opponent on the far end of the clay court behind his house. The ball fell untouched to the ground. So did Darren. His playing partner rushed to call 911, but the paramedics were unable to revive him. Darren Horowitz died of a heart attack in his own backyard.

The following Saturday evening, Greg returned to his apartment from a solitary overnight camping trip to find a red minivan occupying his parking space. He'd gone back and forth a few times with his landlord about others using his spot. It wasn't until he saw the license plate that he realized who owned the vehicle.

DGNTY.

Ambrose and Allen were in the front seats, dozing. They wore dark suits, ties, and white dress shirts. Greg tapped on the driver's-side window.

"Ambrose, what are you doing here?"

Ambrose scrambled to open his door. "I'm sorry, Greg, we didn't know when you'd be home. I tried calling you several times."

"I was out in the woods all day. No cell service. What's so urgent?"

Instead of answering, Ambrose asked, "Do you mind if we come in?"

The brothers helped Greg unload his camping gear from his car, and soon Ambrose and Allen were seated on Greg's couch. Greg sat tiredly in his recliner.

Ambrose spoke. "The Horowitz funeral was this morning, as I'm sure you're aware."

"I wasn't." Greg didn't make much effort to mask his annoyance at having his evening interrupted. "But go on."

"Oh. Well, everything came off nicely. The service was well attended. Private burial at Bluebird Meadows—again, flawless."

Ambrose glanced at his brother, who lowered his head sullenly.

"We . . . we ran into some trouble right after that. We were loading some of the flower bouquets into the hearse when Russ Ginsburg started chatting with us. Do you know Russ?"

"I don't."

"He's new around town. Only lived here for about a year, as I recall. It might be more like two years now that I think about it. Do you know, Allen?"

"Two, I think."

"Let's say somewhere between one and two years, guys. Will that work?"

Neither man seemed to notice the edge in Greg's voice. Ambrose continued, "He talked with us for a few minutes. Just general town stuff at first. Then he asked about the cemetery. He said he'd heard we were opening up a new slate of burial plots."

"Where did he hear that?"

"I have no idea! He said he wanted to buy plots for himself and his wife."

"What did you tell him?"

"I didn't tell him anything. I mumbled something about needing to get to an appointment. Allen and I jumped in the hearse and pulled away without another word!" Ambrose ran his fingers through his hair. "That's not the end of it. This afternoon we've received several phone calls. I think they're related to Russ's question. About the cemetery."

"You *think* the calls are about the cemetery? You don't know?"

Ambrose shook his head. "We didn't answer after the first call. That one was bad. It was Jane Lerner. She said she'd heard that Cotterman had some room available and she was very interested in making a purchase right away. I said we hadn't made a decision about how we're handling things yet. She didn't like that answer. She persisted in trying to purchase a plot, but I held my ground." Ambrose looked at Allen, who gave him an encouraging nod.

"Yeah, but you also confirmed the rumor that Cotterman has space available."

"Not exactly."

"You told Jane you hadn't made up your mind yet. That basically amounts to confirming it."

Ambrose's shoulders slumped forward. "I guess that's true. I hadn't thought of it that way."

"So . . . it sounds like the cat's out of the bag." Greg looked the brothers over and tried to size up their intentions. "What are you gonna do now?"

Allen spoke unexpectedly. "That's why we're here. Ambrose tells me you've got some ideas that might help us."

"I—I mean—" Greg bristled at the idea that the brothers were looking to him for an answer. "I don't really have anything earth-shattering. It's like I told Ambrose the other day. You really only have two ways to go about this. You can sell the plots the old-fashioned way—first come, first served —or you can do some sort of waiting list."

"I don't see how we could possibly sell them outright. Not

now. There's no way to be fair about it now that word has gotten out. It would be an absolute mess!"

"Yes, but you two would stand to make a hefty profit out of it."

"Money is not my main concern here, Greg. I'm much more interested in maintaining the dignity of our business and the respect of our clients."

"Fair enough. So then it's a waiting list. Your own little version of Oklahoma."

"What do you mean by that?"

Ambrose interjected. "I'm uncomfortable with that idea."

"What idea?" Allen asked.

"I don't really see how you can go about it any other way, Ambrose. If there's a better idea out there, I sure don't know what it is."

"Will someone please explain what you're talking about! What is Oklahoma?" Allen stood up. He was not as tall or as slim as his brother, but he had the same long forehead and dark eyes.

Greg waited for Ambrose to speak, but the funeral director was rubbing his temples as if to smooth away his troubles.

"You guys can open up a waiting list and allow anyone who's interested to sign up. The first six people on the list to die get the spots. Everyone's on equal footing. Everyone has an equal chance to get in. Like the Oklahoma Land Rush."

Allen returned to his seat. "Oh. Yes. I remember talking with Ambrose about that."

"But how would we even get started?" Ambrose asked.

No one spoke for a time, mulling over ideas. Greg walked into the kitchen for a glass of water. As he was coming back, he said, "Here's a thought. What if you hold an informational meeting? Get the word out that anyone who's interested should show up. Then, you guys can use the meeting to explain everything and give everyone a chance to sign up. It's fair. It's dignified."

"Seems reasonable," said Ambrose.

"And as an added bonus, you may find that dealing with it out in the open works to your advantage."

"What do you mean?" asked Allen.

"If as many people want these spots as you guys think, it may scare some of them off to see all of the competition in one room at the same time."

"Competition," Ambrose scoffed. "I definitely don't like that terminology."

"Call it whatever you want, but I'm thinking it might convince some people to drop out. Maybe even enough to where you only have six people left. Then you've solved your whole problem in one swoop!"

"If only." Ambrose wasn't yet convinced.

"Well, guys." Greg dropped back into his chair and set his glass of water on the coffee table. "That's all I got for you. If you don't think those ideas will work, then I'm afraid you'll have to find some other problem solver."

"We need to talk it over, of course," said Ambrose.

"Of course. Let me know what you decide. Or don't. It's really none of my business anyway."

The Wannamakers left for home, and Greg stowed his camping gear in the spare bedroom before hopping into the shower and then into bed just before midnight.

CHAPTER 4

*B*y Monday, it was obvious that the Wannamaker brothers would have to do something sooner rather than later. Word of the burial plots was spreading fast and far, though Greg didn't know this until he came into work that morning.

Gladys greeted him before he'd completely stepped through the front door. "So did you hear about Cotterman Cemetery?"

"What? That it's a pretty place to put dead people?"

"It's got six new spaces for sale after all these years."

Greg stored his lunch in the compact refrigerator on the counter behind Gladys's desk. "Technically they're not new. Just unused."

"So you do know about it."

"Ambrose mentioned it to me. How did you hear?"

"How could I not? Lots of folks are up in arms about it."

"What does that mean? People are angry?"

"Some are."

"What's there to be angry about?"

Her desk phone rang.

"Greg! Don't you realize that some folks have been trying to get a spot in Cotterman for decades?"

The phone rang again, but Gladys whirled around in her chair and pounded the hold button.

"Shouldn't you answer that?"

"Oh, they can listen to some classical music for a few minutes."

"If you say so."

"Anyway, some people are upset, but most are thrilled about the chance to get in. That's what I'm hearing. It's really livened things up around here. I got breakfast at the Blue Dot this morning, and most of the regulars in there were talking about it. Everyone wants to know what the deal is."

"The deal?"

"Who gets the burial plots? I know of several people ready to pay a lot of money for them right away."

"Ambrose and Allen aren't looking at this from a financial perspective."

"What do you mean?"

"I think they're more concerned about finding a way to sell the space that's fair to everyone who's interested."

"Like how?"

Greg opted not to tell her about the plan he'd suggested to the brothers, since they hadn't made up their minds yet. Gladys was friendly and a fantastic employee, but she wasn't shy about gossip. He started down the hall toward his office. "I'm sure they'll come up with something. Don't forget that phone call. A person can only stand so much hold music, you know?"

By late that afternoon, Greg was nearly convinced that Ambrose had not been overreacting. Six of Greg's eight patients that day mentioned the Cotterman plots, and five out of those six told Greg they wanted a plot for themselves.

On Tuesday, as Greg sat outside his office building eating lunch, Ambrose called with an update. Inquiries from the townsfolk were unrelenting. The brothers would be holding an informational meeting that Friday in the Hunt

Chapel for anyone interested in buying one of the six burial plots.

The rest of the week slipped past. Greg typically got his Friday dinners from a roadside pizza and wings place thirty minutes out of town—the garlic cheese bread alone made the drive worthwhile. It had become his tradition to pick up his meal and return to his apartment for an evening movie or book.

On his way back tonight, he slowed as he drove past the Cotterman Funeral Home and Memorial Gardens. It seemed that every parking space was taken. He'd only seen the lot this full at a handful of funerals, and he wondered how the number of vehicles outside compared to the number of people sitting inside.

He realized that he'd slowed his car to nearly a stop and was staring at the building. He parked along the road just past the vehicles of several other late arrivers and hustled inside to see the crowd for himself.

The chapel was full. A few empty seats were scattered through the first few rows, and about twenty people stood in the back. Though this wasn't a funeral, to Greg it felt oddly similar to one. Ambrose stood behind the podium onstage looking weary and unhappy as he listened to a short, hunchbacked man in a green cardigan speak in raspy tones.

"It seems to me that you're trying to please everybody, and that's just not realistic. What was it Abraham Lincoln said about pleasing the people?"

Ambrose hesitated, unsure if the man expected an answer. "I don't know."

"Well, the point is you can't please everybody." The man was standing at his seat about a quarter of the way back on the right side of the chapel. "There's only six spots, and I don't really see why my wife and I shouldn't be able to purchase two of them. I've got my checkbook right here. I'm ready to pay you right now, if that's what you want."

"You think you're the only one here ready to shell out?" Whoever yelled this didn't stand up. "You think your money is any better than mine? I'll bet I could double whatever you're gonna pay. Triple!"

"Ladies and gentlemen!" Ambrose cut in. "Please! Let's hear from you one at a time, as I said before."

Greg saw Allen standing in the rear right corner near the audio-video equipment. He went over and greeted Allen in a forceful whisper as the man in the cardigan continued making his case.

"How's it going so far?"

"Awful." Allen was leaning against the back wall with his arms crossed tightly on his chest.

"Yeah, I kinda sensed that. I didn't realize you guys were gonna open it up for public discussion."

"Neither did we. It just sort of happened. Ambrose was in the middle of explaining that we haven't made a decision about what to do with the plots when someone just shouted out at him."

"Who was it? Do you know?"

The man in the cardigan was still talking, but the voice from across the room interrupted again.

"I think your time is up, Lyle! If not, it should be!"

Allen pointed. "Him."

Greg couldn't see who it was.

"So where do things stand right now?" he asked.

"Everyone's just taking turns giving their opinion. It's a mess! I can tell my brother is about to lose it up there. He was already really nervous about running the meeting, but this is making it so much worse."

"Really? I thought he was OK with public speaking. Running all those funerals over the years?"

"That's basically following a script. The same one my father used when he was in charge. This is definitely not the same."

A curly-haired woman near the front raised her hand. "Can I make a suggestion?" It was Jane Lerner.

Jane was short, but she spoke strongly and clearly. "I had a thought just now, and I wanted to share it. Perhaps we should consider coming up with a set of criteria to determine those who are the right fit for Cotterman."

"Criteria?" Ambrose asked.

"Yes. We all understand how important this cemetery is to our town. Emmitsville is a beautiful, wonderful place to live, and the Cotterman Memorial Gardens are a key part of that. I'm sure we can all agree that only those of the utmost character and integrity should be buried here. This place is a representation of our town that will last for centuries after we're all gone!" She pursed her lips, satisfied that she'd dispelled any possible argument.

"You might *think* everyone agrees with that, but you're wrong." The one who had been shouting out stood to his feet, and Greg was finally able to recognize him: Alec Ruttiger. "I don't agree. Not at all. In fact, I think that may be the most jackassed idea I've heard in a long time."

"I beg your—"

"How do you plan to determine who fits your *criteria*? Are you gonna decide that, Jane?"

Jane's confidence appeared to crack slightly. "Well, no. Not necessarily—"

"Is it just the big sins that will disqualify people—like murder and adultery? Adultery will take out more than half the room!" A rumble of whispers arose in the audience. "Do we go down a couple notches and include drug use? Draft dodging? Insider trading? Those would whittle it down even further! What about things like pride and condescension, Jane? Do those count? If they do, you just might be in trouble!"

Jane wilted—Greg even thought she might cry. Instead,

she pursed her lips more tightly and sat down next to her red-faced husband.

"OK then!" Alec shouted, glaring at Jane. "That's settled. Next idea!" He sat down.

Greg silently urged Ambrose to retake control of the meeting, but Daniel Dowager, a nearly bald man in tan slacks and a plaid polo, walked to the podium without asking.

"I think we're approaching this thing from the wrong perspective."

"Yeah, no kidding!" Alec again.

"Instead of talking about ways to decrease the number of people trying to get into Cotterman, why don't we think of ways to increase the number of plots? We probably can't make enough for everyone, but we can certainly get more than six."

"Where are you gonna get the land to do that?" By now, people were talking out at will.

"I'm not talking about getting more land. I'm talking about creating more burial plots out of the land that's already there—and not just the new plots. It's a big cemetery. Let's think outside the box here, people!"

"What else can we do?"

"I don't know exactly, but if I learned anything in my career in plastics it's that you have to be willing to reinvent the wheel sometimes. What are our options?" He stepped back from the podium and waited.

"There's space in between the plots that are already there. What if we used that?"

"But then we'd have to use smaller headstones. And everywhere you walked, you'd be stepping on someone!"

Ambrose took over the microphone. "We . . . we can't do that. The burial plots are already so close together that this would compromise their structural integrity."

"What about stacking the bodies?"

"Excuse me?"

"I mean digging deeper and burying more than one person in a single plot?"

"That might work for families," said someone else in the audience, "but I sure as heck don't want to spend all of eternity with some stranger on top of me!"

A few people chuckled.

"What if we bury people vertically so we can fit more than six?"

"You mean bury them standing up?"

"Sure! Why not?"

"Allen, could you do that?"

Most everyone in the room looked toward the back corner where Allen and Greg were standing.

Allen nodded and shrugged at the same time. "I guess so."

"That's not gonna get us the number we need!" said someone else. "At best, we might get like fifteen or twenty spots."

"Could we recycle older plots? I mean like the *real* old ones from a hundred years ago?"

Ambrose shook his head. "We'd have to get permission from the family to disinter the remains that already reside there."

No more ideas were forthcoming. Daniel Dowager returned to his seat, disappointed that they hadn't reinvented the wheel.

Ambrose looked across the room as if waiting for further input from the crowd. When no one offered any, he spoke. "Well, it seems that we've reached the end—"

"Wait a second!" said Alec.

"Yes, sir? Mr. Ruttiger?"

"You're not gonna talk about the mammoth-sized elephant standing smack-dab in the middle of the room?"

"I'm afraid I don't understand."

Alec turned slightly so those in the rows behind him could

see his face. "How are you going to decide who gets the last six spots?"

Ambrose looked toward Greg and Allen as though seeking help.

"As I said at the beginning, the purpose of tonight's meeting was merely to gauge the level of interest in the burial plots."

"I'd say the interest is pretty damn high. Don't tell me you dragged us all out here just to say you don't know what you're going to do."

"Well, we—we have discussed one possible alternative, but—but I'm not sure . . ." Ambrose interrupted himself with a deep swallow.

Oklahoma, Greg thought. *There's no other way to be fair*.

"So what is it? What's your plan?"

"We have discussed creating a waiting list. Anyone who is interested in purchasing one of the six plots can put their name on the list."

"Who gets to be at the top of the list?" It was Jane Lerner, recovered from her earlier embarrassment.

"It—it wouldn't work as a waiting list in the traditional sense. The idea would be that everyone on the list is on equal footing. No one has any sort of preferred status."

The crowd mumbled.

"When someone from the list passes away, they are awarded one of the plots. We won't accept any prepayments. Only when the plot officially belongs to them will we accept the money from their estate."

The room went silent until Alec broke in.

"So . . . first six to die get in. Is that it?"

Ambrose nodded solemnly.

Alec shrugged. "All right. Just want to know where I stand."

"Does anyone have any questions about this plan?" Ambrose ventured.

Several spoke out.

"I like it. Seems like a fair way to handle things."

"It's a little morbid, but I guess it will work."

"How do we get on this list?"

Ambrose's shoulders relaxed when he saw that the idea had landed positively with most of the crowd. He sounded eager to please. "We will distribute a form sometime next week. Anyone who wants to be on the list should fill it out right away." He surveyed the room once more. "OK, then. It seems this meeting is over. Thank you all for coming and for your understanding. We will make those forms available as soon as we can."

As the townsfolk filed out of the chapel, with hushed conversations and calculating looks, Greg and Allen worked their way toward the front. Ambrose was slumped in a chair on the first row.

"It didn't go exactly as we hoped, but it wasn't a disaster, right?" Allen offered.

"Not quite a disaster, but darn close," said Ambrose sulkily. "Good to see you, Greg. I didn't think you'd be here."

"I decided to check in. I think you guys did great. Most of the fireworks came from Alec. He's a hothead anyway. Sometimes I think he's trying to relive his glory days." Greg tried to sound upbeat.

"I suppose."

"I mean, even just now as I was watching folks leave, I didn't see a lot of angry faces. People seem more thoughtful than anything else."

Ambrose stood and loosened his tie. "I'm not surprised."

"Really?"

"You know what everyone's thinking, don't you?" Ambrose adopted this condescending tone every so often, and it irked Greg.

"I assume they're thinking they want one of those six spots."

"Yes, but they're also wondering who's most likely to die first. Who stands the best chance of getting into Cotterman?"

Greg pictured the crowd as he walked to his car. Ambrose was right. For a group of people accustomed to getting what they wanted when they wanted it—at whatever cost—this was an unfamiliar situation.

They would just have to wait and see whose number came up first.

CHAPTER 5

*A*rriving at his apartment with his cold pizza and garlic bread, Greg saw a gray sedan in his designated parking space. *How hard is it to put up a few signs to mark the guest spots? I'm getting really tired of—*

Then he pulled close enough to make out the car more clearly in the dingy light of the streetlamp. A ballerina figurine dangled from the rearview mirror and a red bumper sticker instructed the reader to *LOVE MORE, BUY LESS*.

Summer.

Of all the deaths at which Dr. Greg had been present over the years, the one that most caught him by surprise was the death of his own marriage. To be precise, his marriage wasn't technically dead. He and Alicia had never divorced, but their union had existed in a persistent vegetative state for fifteen years. For most of that time, their daughter Summer had been the life support keeping their family breathing.

Greg parked his car along the road and walked inside. She was in his recliner with her phone in hand, scrolling.

"Oh! Dad! You're here!"

Greg closed the front door and set his uneaten dinner on the coffee table. "I am. So are you, apparently."

She stood up and wrapped her arms around his neck,

leaning her head snugly on his chest. "Yes! It's so good to see you. I got in a bit earlier than I thought. Sorry."

"You're not kidding! Like a week early."

"What do you mean? It was this week. I'm on my way to Kelly's wedding and you said I could stop by. I gave you the dates."

"I must be mixed up. I really thought it was next week."

"Oh no! This doesn't mess up your plans, does it?"

"Summer, it's me we're talking about. I rarely have plans. The whole weekend is yours. I've even got pizza and garlic bread."

"I already ate, and unfortunately it won't be the whole weekend. I'm supposed to be at Kelly's house by tomorrow night. I'm the maid of honor. Got a lot to do before the wedding."

When Greg walked out of his kitchen ten minutes later with a steaming cup of Earl Grey, Summer was sitting on the couch with her legs tucked beneath her like when she was a girl. He handed her the tea gingerly.

"Thanks, Dad."

Greg settled into his recliner and watched her cool the tea with soft breaths. She'd changed into flannel pajama pants and an oversized T-shirt right after Greg brought her suitcase in from the car. Her light red hair was longer than when he'd last seen her, but her freckled grin was the same as ever.

She looked up from her mug as though she could sense him watching her. "So?"

Greg exited his nostalgic reverie. "So?"

"How's life in Emmitsville?"

"Emmitsville is . . . it's about the same as ever. Strange but mostly peaceful."

"I'm not surprised. People around here have way too much money and time on their hands. Why aren't they putting their wealth to better use? It's a shame."

"Still on a crusade to change the world before you're thirty?"

"Yup."

"And tell me again how that works with a degree in literature?"

"Dad! Really?"

He could see in her eyes that he'd wounded her a little. "Sorry. That sounded way more sarcastic than I meant it to."

"It's OK. The joke gets old after a while."

"I'll retire it. How's that?" She nodded. "But you can't blame me for being a little disappointed. I still think you would've made a great doctor."

"I'm graduating this year, Dad. I'd say that ship has sailed."

"What about your love life?"

"Excuse me?"

"I mean . . ." He was frustrated by how he was stumbling through the conversation. "Any boys I should know about?"

"No, Dad. No 'boys' as of now. Too busy trying to change the world, remember?"

"That's right. Good for you. How's your mother?"

"She's great. Working as hard as ever."

"Is Hillsborough Academy still treating her all right?"

"For sure. Their history department was just listed in the top ten for the state of New Hampshire."

"That's fantastic! She loves what she does, doesn't she?"

They chatted until the pauses in the conversation grew longer and they were both yawning. They hugged good-night.

The next morning Greg was up in time to fry pancakes and bacon before Summer woke. She stumbled from the spare bedroom and sat across from him at the narrow table in the corner of his small kitchen.

"What time do you need to head out today? Can you hang around?"

"I've got three more hours of driving, but I can hang back till probably midafternoon. What did you have in mind?"

"I thought we could grab lunch at the Blue Dot later, and maybe go for a bike ride before that."

"You're still into riding, huh?" She popped a piece of bacon in her mouth.

"I don't get out as much as I used to, but I try to fit a ride in about once a week. Good for the cardiovascular system, you know." He winked at her past his coffee mug as he took a gulp. "It's supposed to be a beautiful fall day here. It'd be a shame to let it go to waste."

"What am I going to ride?"

"I've got your bike in the storage shed."

"Dad! Are you kidding me? The one from when I was in junior high?"

"I'm pretty sure I got it for you in ninth grade."

"It'll be too small."

Greg set his syrup-stained plate in the sink. "Let's find out!"

He wrangled the bike out of the shed and wiped it down with an old rag while Summer finished her breakfast and got dressed. When she came through the sliding glass door from the kitchen, he waved his hand triumphantly.

"What do you think?"

She took the handlebars and swung one leg over the seat.

"Not bad. Not bad."

"I guess you haven't grown up as much as you thought."

They biked down his street, then several blocks over to a tree-lined section of sidewalk that extended a quarter mile to the north before gently curving out of view. He stopped in front of a green sign: *Fred McGowan Rail Trail*.

"What's this?" Summer asked.

"They put this in last summer. There used to be a logging railroad that ran down from the hills east of here and went right through town on out toward Scranton. The railroad hasn't been in use for decades, so they repurposed it."

"Thanks to Fred McGowan?"

"Yes, but that's the funny part. Fred McGowan was probably one of the most un-outdoorsy people around. I'm pretty sure the only time he ever went outside was to get from his car to his house or some restaurant. He was massively overweight. When he died, he donated money to the town and this is how they used it. Makes me wonder what ol' Fred would think if he knew. It kinda cracks me up."

"At least they put it toward something beautiful. This looks amazing."

"Yeah, I really like the trail. I come out here quite a bit."

They rode side by side at a leisurely pace, enjoying the crisp October air and the changing tints of the leaves.

"Doctor! So good to see you!"

The trail ran behind a section of single-story homes on the northern edge of town—one of the valley's more modest neighborhoods. A woman was leaning on her back fence and waving at Greg and Summer.

"Good to see you too, Starlight." Greg dismounted from his bike and held it up by the handlebars.

She was tall—taller than Summer but not quite taller than Greg—and shapely, though on the verge of being underweight. Her bombshell-blond hair swung past her shoulders. She had blue eyes, and a face that was pinched and faded just enough along the edges to reveal the impacts of time and gravity.

Starlight turned toward Summer and extended her hand over the fence. "And good to see you, young lady whom I've never met but am thrilled to get to know!"

"This is my daughter, Summer." The two women shook hands. "Summer, this is Starlight Goodwell."

"Ah! This is Summer! I've heard a lot about you. Nice to finally see you in person."

"Nice to meet you, Mrs. Goodwell."

"Now, Summer, your father will tell you that I'm generally a kind, gracious person. But if you ever call me Mrs. Goodwell again, I don't think we can be friends. Which is a tremendous tragedy because I really want to be your friend! It's Starlight from now on, if you don't mind."

"Oh! OK."

Summer looked flustered, and Greg felt badly for her. "Summer is visiting me for the day. We're out enjoying the scenery."

"I see that. I was just trying get these dang weeds out of my flower garden, but those sneaky little devils are wearing me out!"

"Isn't it late in the season to be trying for a flower garden?"

Starlight narrowed her eyes. "Do I try to tell you how to do your job, Doctor?"

"I wasn't aware that gardening is your job."

Her face widened into a smile. "It's not, thankfully. That would be a sad state of affairs for the world's flower population. You're much better at your job. I'd say you're one of the best doctors in town!" She winked at Summer. "Oh! Wait! You're the *only* doctor in town. That's why you get so many customers. You've got a monopoly!"

"Not quite."

"Yes, but the other medical practices here don't have the customer base that you do."

"That might be true."

"Speaking of your customer base, I heard a bunch of them are jumping in on this Cotterman wait-list thing."

"You heard about that?"

"Hey! I may not be acceptable company to most people around here, but I do have a few connections."

"It was less than 24 hours ago."

"What can I say? People are talking about it—even to me."

Greg set a foot on one of his bike pedals. "It's unique even by Emmitsville standards. I'll say that much about it."

Starlight spoke to Summer. "Your father doesn't much care for our town's sense of propriety and grief."

"I know."

"If only everyone around had the balance and restraint of Dr. Greg Patterson! How much better would this world be?"

For several minutes Starlight peppered Summer with questions about college life, future plans, and romance. Greg steered the conversation to a close.

"I'll see you soon, Starlight."

"Tomorrow's Sunday, you know."

Greg nodded. "Yeah. I'm pretty sure I can make it. I'll let you know if I can't."

"Perfect! Summer, you are a delight to know and a wonderful testament to your father's parenting skills."

"It was so nice to talk with you."

After they'd pedaled a short way down the sidewalk Greg asked Summer, "Well, what did you think of that?"

"Of Starlight? I think she's great!"

"I figured you'd like her. She reminds me of you in some ways."

"But I am curious about her."

"She definitely begs a few questions. She's watching us right now." Greg tilted his head toward Starlight's yard, and Summer slowed down enough to glance back. Starlight was leaning against the fence, watching them ride away.

CHAPTER 6

"*I*s Starlight her real name?"

"No. Her real name's Linda."

"That's unfortunate."

"Summer!"

"I'm kidding! But how creative would her parents have been to name her Starlight?"

"Pretty creative, I suppose. I don't know where the name comes from. For all I know, she gave it to herself."

"So what's her story? Starlight isn't your typical Emmitsvillian."

They'd passed the outskirts of town on Fred McGowan's rail trail and were now surrounded by dense forest.

"Here's what I know," said Greg. "I used to have a patient named Everett Goodwell. One of the wealthiest men in town. About ten years ago, he shocked everyone by divorcing his wife and marrying Starlight."

"Why was that so shocking? It wasn't the first time anyone around here got a divorce."

"But Starlight wasn't from Emmitsville. She'd never even visited before Everett brought her here after their honeymoon. Plus there was the age difference. Everett was in his late seventies; Starlight was in her forties."

"I guess that's a little salacious, but still . . . some of the stories you've told me about this town seem just as bad, if not worse."

"You're right. But her arrival caused a huge stir. People said she was a prostitute who was blackmailing him into a sham marriage. She's an immigrant who swindled him. She's a washed-up movie star looking to get back into some money."

"What's the truth?"

"I don't know exactly. I know she and Everett met in Chicago. That's where she used to live. Other than that, her past is a big mystery to me.

"Everett's first wife left town shortly after the divorce. I haven't heard anything about her since. When Starlight arrived, the town didn't exactly roll out the welcome wagon. I think their anger had to do with *who* Everett stepped out with, not the affair itself. Starlight didn't have any of the credentials that matter to them. Still doesn't."

"It's too bad they're so shallow. She seems like an incredible person."

"Yes. Anyway, as the years went by Everett's health declined and I saw him (and her) much more. He passed away about seven years ago."

"I'll bet that funeral was something else."

"There was no funeral."

"What! Someone from Emmitsville passed up the opportunity for a funeral?"

"Yup. Everett left very specific instructions. A quick cremation and that was it. Starlight buttoned everything up pretty quickly. Sold their big house on the south side of town. Moved into that little place we saw her at today. Been minding her own business ever since. That's what I know about her."

"That's all? Really?"

"Why do you sound surprised?"

"Seems like you two are pretty tight."

"I'm not sure what you mean by that. She loves to talk, but not so much about herself. At least not to me."

"Yeah . . . what's this about Sundays?" Summer probed.

"Oh, that?" Greg felt his face flush. "I sometimes pop over there on Sunday mornings for coffee and a game of cards."

"Really? That sounds like . . . fun."

She sounded playful but he felt irked. He stopped his bike. "What do you mean? What's that face?"

She stopped as well. "I dunno. It's just surprising. A bit out of character for you—Mr. Lone Wolf."

"It's really not a big deal. It's just something that sort of developed over time."

"OK."

Greg felt an urgency to explain himself further.

"She had a string of bad luck about four years ago. She fell on the ice and broke her hip and had to have surgery. Then while she was recovering she developed pneumonia. Once the hospital sent her home, I started swinging by and checking in on her."

"And you just kept it up once she got better." It wasn't a question, and Greg found that even more irksome.

"She doesn't get out much. Like I said, no big deal."

The rail trail continued for a few more miles, but Greg circled them around to cycle back to town.

"How old did you say she is?"

"I didn't, but late fifties."

"That's . . . interesting."

"What's with all the raised eyebrows?"

"She's your age. She's very attractive. You two seem to get along well. It all kinda adds up, doesn't it?"

"Adds up to what?"

"Dad! Why are you being so cagey? She seems like a good match for you. Is there a little more to this relationship than just card games?"

Greg raised one hand as if in surrender. "OK. I get it. This is your way of getting back at me for pestering you about your love life last night. Message received. I'll mind my own business from now on."

"That's not it at all. I'm being totally serious, Dad! It's obvious she's into you. I was just curious if the feeling went both ways. Are you telling me you've never thought about asking her out for a date or something?"

"That's what I'm telling you."

"Why ever not?"

"Summer, I . . . I'm—I'm a married man."

Her shoulders slumped as she pedaled. "Technically."

"Ouch." He tried to say it lightly but couldn't pull it off.

She wasn't looking at him. "I just don't get it. You and Mom."

"I realize our relationship isn't ideal, but it's still a relationship. I'm not going to apologize for feeling a sense of obligation to that."

"I don't expect you to apologize for anything, Dad. Your commitment is honorable, but it's a little ridiculous."

"Ridiculous?"

"Can you honestly tell me that you've never once over the last fifteen years thought about meeting another woman? Not even once?"

"No, I can't say that. I'm human, Summer."

"So? What's the endgame here? For you and Mom?"

"I don't know. You've never put me on the spot like this before. Why now?"

"I love you both, and I just want you to be happy."

"She's not happy?"

"She is—I think she is."

"Has she ever, you know, met anyone else?"

"Not really."

"What does 'not really' mean?"

"I'm sorry. I shouldn't have brought it up. If you tell me

your relationship with Starlight is strictly casual, then I was out of line to suggest anything else. I shouldn't be so nosy."

"We're good, Summer. Always."

They rode without speaking for most of the way to the Blue Dot. Greg fumbled for something to say that would lighten the mood or at least get the conversation rolling again, but she beat him to it.

"What's this you and Starlight mentioned about a big meeting last night?"

"There's a situation shaping up at Cotterman Cemetery." He finished talking her through the details as they pulled up to the diner.

"That's fascinating!" she exclaimed. "What an interesting dilemma for everyone."

"Definitely unique."

"Dad!" She smacked the handlebars and nearly squealed. "Let's go out and look at those burial plots!"

"Really?"

"This is a place that people are literally dying to get into!"

"Don't you have to get going?"

"We can do it real quick after lunch. Can we? Please?"

"Sure." He was rarely able to resist her wide-eyed pleas.

While they ate, Greg was relieved to see that the tension from their talk on the trail had disappeared. Summer chattered away, animated and exuberant in every story. Greg listened and chimed in occasionally.

A short time later they biked into the parking lot of the Hunt Chapel—large, looming, and awaiting the next funeral. The Wannamaker brothers lived in a small home on the far end of the parking lot. To the right of the chapel, an imposing iron gate marked the entrance to the burial ground. A low brick wall extended out on either side of the gate and continued around the perimeter of the property.

Greg and Summer walked through the gate and along a paved pathway. Row upon row of gravesites stretched out on both sides of them. Many of the headstones were large and ornately engraved.

"So where are the last six spots?" Summer was looking around with excitement.

"I don't know exactly. I don't come here often." He turned around several times, trying to get his bearings. "Let's see. Ambrose told me the other day what the numbers were . . . eight forty-something, I think. That would mean . . ." He consulted a small sign in the grass. "We should go this way!"

The path ascended the gentle slope of the hill on which Emmit Willingham had built his famous cemetery. Near the top, Summer stopped and turned back toward the parking lot.

"Breathtaking."

"What is?"

"Seriously, Dad? Just look. The view is amazing!"

Greg turned around. Beyond the sea of headstones and past the towering roof of the chapel, the valley was awash in the burnt reds and deep golds of autumn.

"Not bad."

"Oh! You're such a grump."

They kept climbing until they reached the correct row. Then they turned right and walked along the line of graves. Summer stopped occasionally to read the headstones until they came upon a small patch of grass—undisturbed and unassigned for the time being.

"So this is it?" She asked.

"Yup. This is what all the fuss is about."

"You think it's stupid, don't you?"

"Yes, I do." They stood next to each other, looking at the small plot of land. "But you don't."

"No. Not as much as you do."

"Weren't you just chiding my fellow citizens for being shallow and not using their wealth and power for good?"

She kept looking down at the grass. "Yes, but this feels different to me. This is more . . . real."

Greg laughed. "Real? There's nothing real about this. Every person who's willing to bend over backwards for one of these spots won't even get to enjoy it. They won't know they're here! What's real about that?"

"They'll know it before they go. *When* they go."

"What difference does that make?"

"I think it makes a huge difference, Dad." She sat cross-legged in the grass. "You're right that all these things— funerals, burials, memorials—don't make any difference to the person who's gone, but I don't think that's the point. Maybe it's more about providing some comfort before they're gone. And what about comforting those left behind? Giving them closure?"

He sat down next her. "I think closure is way overrated."

"The people in Emmitsville are self-centered and pretentious. I agree. But on this one point I'm willing to give them a pass. This makes sense to me."

Greg could only shrug.

Summer continued, "Think of it this way. Why do some kids risk their lives to spray-paint graffiti on a cargo train or an overpass?"

"Because they're punks with too much time on their hands?"

"Maybe they're just trying to leave their mark. Deep down, they're grasping for something that shows they were here. They mattered."

"You're telling me the kid who used to spray the word *naked* all over town when I was in college was trying to reach some level of existential significance?"

"Well, maybe not that example specifically, but this is an actual thing, Dad. I'm not just making it up. We talked about it in my psychology class last year."

"Psychology? For a lit major?"

"I had to take it for my liberal arts requirements. It was fascinating! There's this idea that every human being intuitively looks for ways to affirm their own significance. Some people do it through graffiti. Others do it through business. People in Emmitsville do it by getting into Cotterman."

"Among other things."

"Exactly. All of it boils down to our attempts to cope with our impending oblivion. If we can't stay here forever, then at least some part of us can. Somehow, it makes us feel better about leaving. Everybody's got their thing, Dad. Even me."

"I thought you were a believer? On your way to heaven and all that."

"I am, but that doesn't mean the thought of dying doesn't scare the bejeebers out of me like everyone else. You think I don't get freaked out at the thought of not being here?"

"I guess not."

"People believe in Jesus, Buddha, the boogeyman, or nothing at all. That's their choice. But when you get right down to it, we all face the same uncomfortable truth. The other side isn't here. It's something different. We can't see it or study it. It just stands there, waiting for us. If a huge headstone in Cotterman Cemetery or carving our initials on a tree trunk makes it easier to face the darkness, then I say—go for it!"

Greg watched her carefully as she spoke. The tenderness in her eyes. He saw plainly that she believed what she was telling him.

"So, what's yours?"

"My what?"

"Your thing? Your way of—how'd you say it—'coping with impending oblivion'?"

She looked away. "I don't want to say. You'll think it's silly."

"Come on! I promise to be kind."

She hesitated. "Every time I move away from a place, I hide a note in the bedroom I'm leaving behind. Just a little note for the next person who lives there. I tell a little bit about myself and wish them peace and blessing."

"Oh."

"You think it's stupid, don't you?"

"No! Not at all. I had no idea. So, you left a note in your tiny little bedroom when we moved from that awful apartment in Woburn?"

"Well, no. I didn't start doing this until a couple of years after you moved away. I think I was twelve, so it would have been when Mom and I moved from Somerville up to New Hampshire."

"That's interesting. I wonder what my thing is."

She giggled. "Oh, come on, Dad! You know what it is."

"I guess I'll have to think it over a little."

Summer stood abruptly after checking the time on her phone. "I better get going. Still have a drive ahead of me."

They covered the return distance to the parking lot much more quickly than their walk up the hill. Back at Greg's apartment, Summer hugged him tightly before driving away. He lingered on his front step and watched her car until it was out of sight, fragments of the day's conversation ringing in his mind and the ache of seeing her off pulsing in his chest.

CHAPTER 7

*F*or thirty-five days after Darren Horowitz passed away, no one in Emmitsville died. The Wannamaker brothers went about compiling their sizable waiting list, but there wasn't a single fatal event in town—for anyone on the list or otherwise. Many found this unnerving. Some talked about it like a supernatural phenomenon, as if holy water had fallen over the valley during a recent rainstorm and rendered it immune to mortality.

Gladys had a different take.

"It's like we're all together in a giant kitchen with a leaky sink. For years the faucet has released drip after drip of water, but we haven't taken notice. Now, everyone is watching the faucet and fidgeting. We're all waiting for the next drop to pull loose and fall!"

It was the morning of the thirty-sixth day, and Greg leaned on the counter that separated Gladys's workstation from the waiting room. "That's a poetic way to put it, but you're blowing it out of proportion. This so-called dry spell isn't that long."

"How do you know?"

"I'm a doctor. Knowing these things comes with the job."

"Is that so?"

"Mostly. I may have done some snooping on the Bureau of Vital Statistics website last night."

Gladys smirked back. "Ah! There it is."

"The truth is that a small town like Emmitsville can go for a month or even two or three without a single death. And sometimes we have twenty in two weeks! It's all just part of the ebb and flow, you know?"

"Twenty! That would be interesting. It could come down to a photo finish for the last spot in Cotterman. Who died first?"

He looked out the front window at the midmorning walkers. "Just remember this. When it's all over and the excitement dies down, they're just six holes in the ground."

She clicked her computer screen on. "Well, you should hope this dry spell ends soon, or it could put you out of business."

"What do you mean?"

"Haven't you noticed your light schedule? Doctor! You've had more cancellations in the last month than a cheap airline."

"How many cancellations are we talking about?"

"A lot. Remember last Friday? You had one patient. Friday's usually our busiest day."

"What does that have to do with the dry spell?"

She folded her hands together and leaned forward slightly so she could look squarely at him. "The next six people to die get the last six spots in Cotterman. It's *important* to some people to get into that cemetery. So . . . you suddenly start getting lots of cancellations."

"But . . . what you're suggesting is ludicrous!" She kept her hands folded and stared at him blankly. "Gladys! You're not gonna sit there and tell me that people are actually *trying* to die more quickly so they can get into Cotterman?"

"Well, it's not like someone is gonna go and off themself in order to get in." She paused and considered the idea. "At least, I don't think they will. What I *am* saying is that this situation has a lot of people thinking about what's important to them. For some, Cotterman is bigger than living a few extra months or years. Like it or not."

"This is utterly asinine! There are 160 people on this stupid list vying for six spots. Their chances of getting in aren't—"

"How do you know how many are on the list?"

Greg winced and wished he could snatch those last few words out of the air. "I've seen the list. Ambrose showed it to me last week."

"He showed it to you? Is he supposed to do that? Privacy rules or something?"

"Well, he did." Gladys crossed her arms and waited. "Look, the truth is that the waiting list was my idea. Ambrose came to me for help when this all started, and I made the suggestion."

"Interesting."

"I don't know why they came to me, but they did. The waiting list seemed like a good idea in theory."

"It is a good idea."

"Yeah, but if what you're telling me today is accurate, then it's not a good idea. Not at all! Not if it's causing people to lose their minds and give up on their lives. You really think that's what's happening?"

"OK, how about this?" Gladys scrolled for several seconds through her calendar. "Ah! Ernie Wilson. He hasn't been in for a visit in over a month."

"What?" Greg leaned over the counter and looked at her screen. "That can't be right. I need to see him every week!"

"See these red entries? Missed or canceled appointments. Ernie's missed his last four."

Greg shook his head. "Unbelievable."

"If it helps at all, his wife is the one who's been canceling.

In fact, she called a few days ago and canceled the next three appointments."

"Gerry did?" Gladys nodded. "Well, that doesn't surprise me as much. She's . . . she's . . ."

"Yes. She is. Very much so."

Greg drummed his fingers on the counter while Gladys watched him with one eyebrow raised.

"I'm guessing today's schedule is pretty wide open."

"Nothing till two thirty."

"Well, then. I think I'll pop over to the Wilson place for a house call."

When Greg arrived at Ernest and Geraldine Wilson's house, he followed their housekeeper across a cavernous foyer and through French doors to a shaded patio.

"Dr. Patterson is here."

Ernie and Gerry sat at a small round table set for breakfast. The oval patio was bordered with multicolored rose beds. Beyond was a long lawn of deep-green grass and clear, straight mower lines.

Gerry stood up to greet Greg.

"Dr. Greg! So good to see you. We were quite surprised when Annette told us you were at the door." She cupped her hands around one of his and shook it eagerly.

"Good to see you, Gerry. And Ernie." Ernie looked over one shoulder and waved before taking a gulp of orange juice. "I'm sorry for dropping by like this, but I had some open time and thought I'd check in on Ernie. Haven't seen you for a couple of weeks."

"Has it been that long?" Gerry was resting one hand lightly on Greg's arm. Her smile and tone of voice felt suspiciously bright to Greg.

"Yes. It has. Nearly a month, I believe. I didn't want to let any more time slip by without taking a look at you, Ernie."

Gerry sidestepped, placing herself between Ernie and Greg. "Now that you mention it, I do remember that we've missed our last few appointments! Ernie's been doing much better, and there hasn't been such a need for it."

"*Much* better? Is that right?"

"Oh, yes! He's in far less pain and his breathing sounds a lot easier."

Greg tried to move around Gerry. "Ernie, that's . . . that's tremendous. Have you been sleeping better?"

"I suppose." Ernie only turned slightly when speaking to Greg.

"Since I'm here, I'd love to check—"

"Gerry, dear? Would you find Annette and ask her to lay out some town clothes for me?"

Gerry kept smiling. "What's that?" She crouched next to his chair and patted his arm.

"I think I'd like to go into town today. Maybe stop by the library, and then find something to eat. So if you wouldn't mind having Annette lay out some clothes . . . I'll be in shortly, OK?" He patted her arm in return and smiled sweetly.

Gerry hesitated and then stood tall. "Thank you for stopping by, Doctor. I hate to cut your visit short, but it appears we are headed into town. I'll be glad to—"

"Actually," said Ernie, "I'll chat with Dr. Greg a moment. You find Annette, and we can all be on our way soon. Does that sound all right, sweetheart?"

Gerry's smile sank somewhat. "Of course. Thank you, once again, Doctor." She paused at the French doors before closing them behind her.

"Would you like to take a seat?"

Greg pulled out a chair and sat next to the old man.

Ernie held up a crystal carafe. "Orange juice?"

"No, thank you."

Ernie took a sip. "Thanks for stopping by, Doctor. You've always gone out of your way for me. I appreciate it."

"Oh. You're welcome. I hadn't seen you for a while, and I

thought—"

"I know what you thought—what you think. I know why you're here."

"You do?"

Ernie ran his fingers through his hair. "I'm eighty-eight years old, Greg. I've lost many things over the last few years, but my ability to read people isn't one of them."

"I'm not sure I understand."

"You're not just here to check up on me. I know that you're here to . . . *check* . . . *up* . . . on me. You follow?"

Greg didn't answer, but assumed his expression said it for him.

"It's crazy, huh? This town. These people. You think we're all nuts."

"I've never said that."

Ernie chuckled. "Not publicly. Oh! It's OK, you know. I'm not offended. Some of us are nuts. Some of us are mean and nasty. There's a few good ones around here, just don't ask me to name names!"

The old man's candor put Greg at ease. He realized how tense and grumpy he'd been when he first arrived at the house. "I won't."

"You don't need to be worried."

"Ernie, I'm your doctor. I'm supposed to be concerned about your health."

"Of course, but I'm not talking about me." He nodded his head toward the house. "You don't need to be worried about *her*." Again, Greg said nothing. "She's . . . she's a handful. I know that makes her sound like a four-year-old, and in some ways that's not too far from the truth. Don't take me wrong! I love her dearly, and she's always been true to me. For sixty years, she has. We have. There's never been anyone else for either of us. Before we were married or after.

"But if I'm honest, for sixty years it's been one tornado after another with her. Our wedding. Vacations. The kids' schooling. You name it! She dreams big and bold. Always. She never does anything halfway. I've filled more closets and storage units than you can imagine trying to give her all of that. I couldn't tell you why, exactly, because I know I'll never be able to give her enough. Like I said, I love her and . . ." Regret and sadness swept into his eyes. "As much as I've given her—I've let her down a lot too.

"We both put our names on the wait list for Cotterman. I wasn't at the meeting, but she went. She filled out our forms and sent them in right away. It's important to her. Just like all the other things. You follow me?"

Greg nodded.

"But she's not crazy enough to actually do me harm."

Greg raised his hands apologetically. "I never thought that—"

"Yes, you did." Ernie's smile returned. "It's OK! Believe you me. I've wondered about it myself over the last few weeks. I even stopped drinking my orange juice in the mornings."

"Really?"

"Yes, sir. She stopped drinking it. Suddenly, it was grapefruit juice for her instead. I started thinking that over one morning and poured my cup out on those flowers there just to be safe! Did that for nearly a week. The roses are fine, you can see, so I guess I'm in the clear.

"It comes down to this, Doctor. She wants me to get one of those spots. Well, actually, she wants *us* to both get spots, but that's not likely now. She's younger. Healthier. I'm—well, you know how I am, Doc. So, I guess you could say she—*we*— have come to realize that it's OK to relax a little and just let nature take its course. Trudging into town each week to see you isn't going to stop the inevitable, but it might just keep me from giving her one last gift. You follow?"

Greg considered offering an alternative view of the situation, but something about Ernie's talk had sapped any fervor he had for an argument. "Well, promise me you won't go too much longer without coming in to see me. The end of life is inevitable, but pain and suffering aren't."

"Good point, Doc! Like I said, you've always had my best interest in mind. I've never doubted that."

The waiting room was still empty when Greg returned to his office. At her desk, Gladys was flipping through the pages of a cooking magazine. "Were you successful?"

"What do you mean?"

"Rescuing Ernie Wilson from death by appointment cancellation."

"Not really. There's a weird logic with them that's hard to pin down."

"Well, better luck with someone else."

Greg stopped on his way into the corridor and leaned back to look at her. "There's someone else?"

"I'm sure there's plenty of someone elses. In this case, I mean Archie Early."

"What's wrong with Archie?"

She closed her magazine. "Apparently, he's taken up smoking."

"Archie doesn't smoke. Not since I've known him."

"He just started."

"How do you know?"

"I have sources around town, Doctor. You should know that by now."

In his office, Greg tossed a couple of darts and tried to think through Ernie Wilson's way of looking at the world. He kept coming back to the same conclusion: *It's superficial crap! That's all it is.*

He pictured Archie Early smoking his first cigarette at seventy-eight years of age. Archie was a tall man—well over six feet—and exceptionally healthy. He was also talkative and unreservedly friendly. Greg was usually put off by those traits, but Archie made it difficult not to like him.

Greg decided it was time for lunch. After getting his order to go from the Blue Dot, he found an empty bench in Lerner Park. The day was warm and clear. People filled the sidewalks and benches, as if everyone was aware that autumn was breezing past and winter's chill would settle on the valley in the next few weeks.

Greg pulled out his cell phone, ignoring the banner telling him he'd missed three calls from his sister, and dialed up Archie.

"Hello?"

"Hi, Archie. It's Greg Patterson."

"Well, Dr. Greg! How the heck are you?"

"I'm just fine. You?"

"Fine and dandy, sir. Fine and dandy! To what do I owe the pleasure? Not late on a bill, am I?"

"I'm calling to ask you a question."

"Go for it."

"Well," Greg balked. What if Gladys's "sources" were wrong? They weren't usually, but still. "I wanted to ask you something. It's kind of an awkward question."

"You sound downright mysterious."

"No! I'm not meaning to. I just wanted to ask. Are you— have you—started smoking recently?"

Archie laughed loudly, and Greg imagined him slapping his knee. "Well, now! That's not what I expected to hear from you, Doc!"

"So it's not true?"

"Oh, it's true. Sort of."

"What does that mean?"

"Jimmie Walker and me were talking with Alec Ruttiger yesterday and he bet us five hundred dollars each that we couldn't smoke a whole pack in less than twenty-four hours."

"Why would he do that?"

"Who the heck knows? It's Alec. Anyway, Jimmie and me

figured we could prove him wrong and earn some cash, you know?"

"So you are smoking. At least for a day."

"Looks like it."

"You've never smoked before."

"Not once. I've tried just about everything at least one time, but never that. It just never appealed to me."

"But it does now." Greg was straining to keep from sounding judgmental.

"It's more the thought of proving Alec wrong and taking five hundred dollars from him. The smoke is just secondhand. Hey! That's funny, right?"

"So, are you going to win this bet?"

"It's lookin' that way. Only have to smoke two more before four o'clock today. I got a fightin' chance!"

Greg left his bench and threw the paper bag from the Blue Dot in a nearby trash can. He tried to think of how to proceed, but Archie spoke first.

"Now, I want to ask you a question, Greg. How did you know, and why did you call me about it?"

"Um . . ." Greg felt embarrassed that he'd followed the trail of town gossip. "Gladys told me."

"Well, I didn't tell Gladys so someone must have told her."

"Probably so."

"I swear! Just when I think people around here are gonna shut up and mind their own business." If Archie hadn't been chuckling while he said it, Greg might have thought he was upset.

"I called you because I was concerned, Archie. I don't have to tell you how unhealthy smoking is, do I?"

"I suppose not. Still, you coulda brought it up next time I was in your office."

Archie was prodding, and Greg was caught off guard by the man's perception that there was more to it. "I guess I'm just out of sorts right now, if I'm going to be completely honest."

"What's got you out of sorts?"

"The truth is this thing with the Wannamakers and the cemetery is causing some of my patients to . . . to act a little out of the ordinary. That's all."

"And you thought me lighting up a Camel was my way of trying to get into Cotterman. Is that it?"

"It sounds ridiculous now, but yes. The thought had crossed my mind."

"It don't sound ridiculous, Doc. I wouldn't put it past some of my fellow citizens to do something just like that, or worse!"

"Really?"

"Roots run real deep around here. Especially when it comes to that burial ground. A lot of history in there! My mama and pop are in Cotterman. Somehow they convinced old man Emmit to sell them a couple of his own spots from the family plot."

"Willingham?"

"The one and only. They talked him into it shortly after they moved here. I think Emmit only agreed to it to piss off someone in his family. Not sure who.

"I'd be lying if I said I didn't care about getting in there, too, when my time comes. I never found a wife. Got no kids that I know of. All my money is earmarked for this and that once I leave. I figure it'd be nice to rest in peace out there on that hillside. It's got a great view of the valley."

"Yes, it does."

"But I'm in no hurry to shuffle off—I still got plans. Plenty of plans. Heck! I might still get married one of these days. You never know."

Greg had begun walking the eight blocks back to his office. "I'm glad to hear your perspective. Not everyone is so clear-headed about this. It just baffles me."

"Well, of course it does!"

"What do you mean?"

"No offense, but you're only . . . how old are you?"

"I'm fifty-six."

"Yeah. You're only fifty-six. Still too young. You haven't had to square up to death yet."

"I deal with death all the time."

"Yeah, but that's more of a professional thing. You can still keep your distance. At my age, you look at death a little differently. Your mind starts to wander into territory you used to avoid. You start thinking about the end. About your legacy. That sort of stuff. It's not as scary anymore. It's just . . . persistent. You start counting down instead of counting up. You know what I mean?"

Greg thought of Summer's theory about coping with oblivion. "I suppose."

"So I can sorta understand why some folks seem to be going off half-tilt. Like I said, roots can run pretty deep. But you don't have to worry about me! After today, I'm quitting smoking. Cold turkey. I promise."

"I hope so, Archie. Thanks for the chat."

"You betcha, Doc. You keep all those other crazies in line, OK?"

"I'll do my best. Bye now."

Greg pushed open his office door and announced, "Well, as much as I hate to admit it, I think you may be right. Don't let it go to your head."

Behind her counter, Gladys shot to her feet. "You're back! Your sister has been trying to reach you for hours."

Greg looked down at his phone screen. His total of missed calls was now at seven. "She called here just before you walked in." Gladys pulled off her reading glasses. "Oh, Greg. I'm sorry to be the one to tell you, but Sandy couldn't get you. Your father was involved in a serious car accident this morning."

CHAPTER 8

I'm sorry, but he didn't make it.
Greg had uttered statements like this many times over his career. It was never easy or enjoyable, but he approached it the same way he approached every part of his job: with a calm demeanor and a quiet determination to do it well.

Gladys's announcement that day was one of the few occasions when he was the receiver of the bad news rather than the bearer. He responded with the same calmness and determination, though the force of the punch he felt in his gut surprised him.

He immediately booked a flight to Denver and a rental car. After that, he called Sandy. She was wholly distraught, barely able to speak complete phrases through her sobs. Greg did his best to wade through her hysteria and communicate that he would be there as soon as possible.

He landed at Denver International Airport just after five o'clock the next day, then headed straight to the rental-car counter with his carry-on. He was driving toward Denver's southwest suburb of Lakewood as the sun dipped below the mountains to the west. At his father's home—a stucco-covered, two-story model identical to the ones on either side of it—he fished the key out of his jacket and let himself in.

Unsure exactly what to do while he waited for Sandy, he looked around the kitchen and living room as if studying an archaeological site. He examined his dad's handwritten notes on the calendar and the selection of books on a shelf next to the small TV.

"Greg! You're here!"

He hadn't heard the front door open. Sandy slammed it behind her and rushed to throw her arms around his neck.

"I'm so glad to see you! The last twenty-four hours have been just horrid! I still . . ." She started sobbing. "I still can't believe he's gone. Isn't it just surreal?"

"Yes. It's hard to wrap your mind around."

She pulled some tissues from a box next to their father's easy chair. "How are you holding up?"

"I'm OK. Probably still in shock a little. And I'm tired. My first flight left Boston at 6:05 this morning."

"Thank you for getting here so fast. I wish you could have been here last night. I think I might have slept better."

"I'm here now."

Greg looked around the room awkwardly. He had only been to the house twice since his father bought it three years earlier. Sandy, who lived half an hour away, visited often.

"It's so strange to be here and think that he was in this room only yesterday," said Sandy. "Everything is exactly the way he left it."

"Yeah." He stepped toward the kitchen counter. "It's pretty well kept in here. Dad never liked to collect clutter."

"The polar opposite of me!"

Greg noticed a red light flashing on the base unit of the cordless phone. "Looks like he's got voicemail." He tapped the button.

"What are you doing?" Sandy sounded alarmed.

"I'm checking his messages."

"But . . . but that's private. Those are messages for *him*."

"Sandy, we'll be going through a lot of Dad's private things over the next few days. That's part of the process."

She bit her lip as the tears returned. "I know. You're right. It just makes me feel like . . . an intruder."

"I get that, but we've got to bite the bullet."

She nodded. He tapped the button again.

"What's his pass code?"

"I have no idea."

Greg tried *0000*, the house number, and the last four digits of Dad's phone numbers, but failed each time.

"Try *0511*," offered Sandy. "Mom's birthday."

"Oh. Yeah. Of course." He punched in the digits, and the digitized female voice announced that two unheard messages were waiting. The first was the last ten seconds of a recorded sales call. The second message was from a local number.

"Larry, this is Marcia. I just heard from Pastor about what happened to you. I—I don't even know what to say!" Marcia began crying. "I will miss you so much. You've always been so kind to me and to so many others around here. I know God's way is perfect, but . . . but honestly . . . this just doesn't seem right. I feel like you deserved more time." More tears. "I haven't talked to Sandy yet. I'm sure I will soon. And your son. Oh, Larry, I don't remember his name, but I know you've been praying for him for so long. I hope to meet him and encourage him! I will miss you, my friend. Rest in the arms of Jesus now. Tell your bride hello for me. I'm sure she's thrilled to be reunited with you at long last. Bye now."

The voicemail system wanted to know what to do with the message. Though Greg's inclination was to hit *Delete*, Sandy asked him to save it.

"That was weird."

Sandy was still looking around the house with wide, red-rimmed eyes. "What? The voicemail?"

"Yeah. Who's this Marcia? Do you know her?"

"Yes. She attends our church."

"She and Dad were . . . ?"

"They were friends. What's weird about it?"

"She left a voicemail for someone she knew was dead. That doesn't seem odd to you?"

"Just her way of saying good-bye, I suppose."

Greg shrugged stiffly. "What's next? I feel like we should be doing something."

"Did you go see it?"

"See what?"

She pointed at the front window. "Where it happened. On the corner."

"The accident?" She nodded. "I mean . . . I saw it as I was driving in. Was there something I was supposed to notice?"

"I don't know."

"You haven't seen it?"

"No."

"But you drove past to get here."

She shook her head insistently. "No. I came the other direction. I wanted to wait for you. Can we walk down together?"

At the corner of Mesa Verde Avenue and Wadsworth Boulevard, they watched silently as an unbroken chain of vehicles zipped past on Wadsworth.

Greg spoke first. "Traffic. One of the reasons I don't miss living in the city!"

Sandy was staring at the utility pole by the sidewalk. Someone had stapled a page from a middle-school yearbook to the wood. On the ground were several candles and a white teddy bear.

"This is where it happened?"

Sandy started crying again as she nodded. When her emotion subsided enough for her to talk, she said, "The police said Dad was turning left onto Wadsworth. It was just after eight a.m. Rush hour. I don't understand why he didn't go a different way. You know how he felt about left turns."

"He'd reroute himself just to avoid them!"

"That's why I'm so surprised. This road is super busy in the mornings. There's no stoplight—practically impossible to make a left. Why on earth did he try it? When I first got my license he told me over and over, 'Only pull out when you're ready. You're the driver! Don't let anyone else in the car pressure you into it.'"

"Yeah. He told me that, too."

"He was hit by a box van." She held her hand to her midsection and looked stricken. "Sorry. I just can't let myself think about . . . what it must have been like. I know you're used to that, but it's very difficult for me."

"Sandy! Just 'cause I work in medicine doesn't mean I'm immune to something like this."

"I know." She touched the edge of the yearbook page tenderly. "This is beautiful."

"What is?"

"All of this." She gestured toward the items at the utility pole. "Looks like some of Dad's students came over here yesterday. I had to call the principal at his school and tell her. Oh, dear Lord! How awful that must have been for those kids to hear the news!"

His hands in his jeans pockets, Greg stared at the utility pole. "I dunno. I've always thought things like this were . . . kind of inappropriate."

"Why would you say that?"

His better sense told him to steer the conversation in a new direction, but he didn't. "It just seems to make the whole thing so obvious. I mean, why don't they put up a huge sign that says, *Someone died here today*?"

She looked wounded. "I . . . I never think about it that way! The pictures. The messages. It's all so sweet and . . . and . . ." She lowered her head into her hands and wept.

Greg rubbed her shoulder lightly. "I'm sorry. I should keep my mouth shut."

"Not necessarily. If that's how you really feel, then . . . I mean . . . I guess we just look at things differently."

"We always have." He felt the fatigue from his travel pulling on him. "Listen, I'm beat. Let's head back and talk about tomorrow. Sound good?"

They trudged the three blocks back to Dad's house as Sandy rehearsed the details for Greg.

"The funeral is on Thursday at eleven a.m. The viewing is tomorrow. The family—we go first at two o'clock. The public viewing is three to five. Lipman and Sons are taking care of all of that for us."

"Lipman . . . Lipman. Why does that sound familiar?"

"It's the same place that did Mom's funeral."

"Really? That's . . . weird."

She looked at him nervously. "You think we should've gone with someone else? I just figured it made sense."

"I'm sure they'll do great. They did fine with Mom's funeral."

She still looked uneasy. "Greg, I need you to speak up if you're not happy with something. We don't have to do things my way."

"Sandy. Stop freaking out."

"I'm not freaking out. I just want to be sure—"

"I think everything's fine. Let's just stick with what we decided—you handle the funeral arrangements, and I'll deal with all the paperwork and financial stuff. I think that makes sense."

"I do have a favor to ask."

"Go for it."

"Can you write the obituary? We need it for the newspaper and the funeral home website."

"Um . . . sure. I can do that. How long does it have to be?"

"I don't know. I guess you'll have to look it up."

Greg woke up early the next morning and spent several hours trying to pull together an obituary for his father. Most of the writing he had done in his life had been academic in nature, and he found this task to be particularly elusive. "It's a fool's errand to try to capture the essence of a person's entire existence in a couple of cute paragraphs," he said to himself. He flirted with the idea of sending this thought in a text message to Sandy but decided against it.

"Having a sibling is like sitting next to someone on a long flight. It's awkward, but you know you're going to be with them for a while so you have to make the best of it."

He opted not to send that one either.

After carving out only a couple of sentences by noon, he closed his laptop and dressed in a suit coat, tie, and slacks. He had plenty of time to swing by the insurance agent's office on his way to the viewing.

The agent helped Greg fill out paper work for the life-insurance policy and gave him an overview of next steps. Greg and Sandy would receive equal portions of the death benefit—a term Greg had always found ironic.

He finished at the insurance agency sooner than he'd anticipated. With forty-five minutes left before he was to meet Sandy at the funeral home, Greg sat in his rental car at a red light and mentally fidgeted over what to do with himself. Looking around, he realized how close the insurance office was to his childhood home. When the light turned green, he turned left.

Greg slowed down once he reached his old block. One. Two. Three. Four houses up on the right. There it was, looking much the same as it had the last time he'd been by. The trees were taller. Someone had taken out a couple of the rosebushes in front. But the paint color hadn't changed, and it looked like the backyard privacy fence was the same one Greg and his dad had installed thirty-seven years before, the summer after Greg's freshman year of college.

Greg rolled down the road a little further before pulling to the curb. He got out of the SUV and walked around to lean on the back bumper. He was trying to decide whether to walk closer to the house when he heard a small, high voice call out behind him.

"Dipper! Dipper! Here, boy! Come here, Dipper!"

A young girl was sitting cross-legged in her yard with a wire cage on the grass in front of her. The cage was empty and the door was open.

"Dipper! Here, boy!" She tried unsuccessfully to whistle. When she saw Greg, she stopped yelling and clammed up with embarrassment.

Greg tried to put her at ease. "Hello."

"Hi."

"Did you lose your pet?"

"Yes. His name is Dipper. He's a rabbit." Her enthusiasm about the animal outweighed any shyness she was feeling. "He got away last night. I think I left the cage open on accident."

"Oh. I'm sorry about that. Has he ever gotten out before?"

"No."

"Do rabbits know how to come back to their cages if they get out?"

She shrugged. "Mom said he might recognize my voice if he's hiding somewhere 'cause he's scared. She looked up on the dot com, and it said so."

Greg scanned the neighborhood but didn't see any signs of Dipper. "He's been gone all night, huh?" She nodded. "Well, I really hope you find him."

"He'll come back! I believe in magic!"

She was still calling out for Dipper as Greg got back into his car and started it up.

CHAPTER 9

He knew he wasn't supposed to go in her room and bother her. Dad said it at breakfast to him and his sister. It had been a bad night. Just like the night before and the night before that. She needed to be alone to rest.

He hated bad nights and he hated that she was alone. He couldn't remember the last time she'd come out of her room.

The afternoon TV shows looked dumb. It was hot outside. Sandy was holed up in her room reading.

He hated reading and he hated being bored.

He looked at his latest Erector Set creation on the coffee table. She always looked so happy and excited when he showed her what he'd made. Maybe that's what she needed today: to feel happy and excited for a change.

Holding the metal contraption, he pushed open her bedroom door. It was stuffy inside. All of the curtains were closed. He waited for his eyes to adjust to the darkness. The only light in the room came from the hallway behind him and the narrow gap between the curtains and the windowsill. He tried not to breathe through his nose. He didn't know what the smell was, but he didn't like it.

He stepped forward as quietly as he could. He could now

see clearly enough to make out the shape of the bed and the form of her body under the blankets. She hadn't lifted her head to greet him like she usually did.

He hesitated. Sleep was good for her. She needed to rest. It had been a bad night. He wasn't supposed to bother her. He knew it.

But it had been so long since he'd seen her out of her room or even sitting upright in her bed.

"Mom?"

He was careful to say it only slightly louder than a whisper.

She didn't answer.

He would try only one more time. "Mom?"

He took a few mini steps closer. The room held just enough light for him to see her face.

Her eyes were closed. Some of her hair had fallen over one side of her face, covering her cheek and part of her mouth.

Every time this scene would replay itself in his mind over the years, he would remember two thoughts that came to him at that moment.

First—the pain he usually saw on her face was gone.

Second—the strands of hair near her mouth and nose were completely still. His young mind interpreted this observation as if by instinct.

He stood and stared at her as the realization settled on him. His mom was dead.

"Greg! What are you doing in here?" his father whispered as he stepped past. Greg's father knelt beside the bed and leaned in toward his mother's face, putting his hand on her shoulder. Then he leaned backward and raised a fist to his mouth to smother the anguished exclamation.

"Oh, dear Lord! Please! It's too soon!"

He rushed to the bedroom door. "Dorothy! Dorothy! Please get in here! I think—"

Sandy appeared in the doorway first. "What's wrong? What happened?"

His dad had returned to the bedside and was squeezing his mom's hand.

Greg's grandmother and sister approached the bed cautiously. The three of them, huddled around the bed, let out shouts of shock and grief.

"Why wasn't I in here? I should have been in here. I just stepped out to fix a sandwich!"

"Oh dear Lord!"

"Mommy!"

Greg remained where he was standing. Sandy looked at him and extended her arms.

"Oh, Greg! Are you OK? Come hug me."

He turned his back on the bed and walked across the hall to his own room, where he shut the door.

$\mathcal{T}$he only other family members who showed up for the early viewing were Uncle Randy and Aunt Larissa. They arrived at the funeral home just after Greg and Sandy.

When Sandy wrapped her arm around Greg's and started toward the reposing room, he realized what she had in mind.

"What's wrong?" She felt him holding back.

"I . . . I think I'd prefer to go in alone." He didn't want to look at Sandy directly because he knew what was coming.

"You . . . do? Why?"

He pulled his arm away. "It's just . . . I feel like it's . . . a personal thing. You know?" He could see the sadness creeping from her lips up to her eyes.

"Oh, Greg! I'm not sure I can go in there by myself."

He fidgeted with the sleeve of his suit jacket. "I'm not

trying to make this difficult. I'd just prefer to see Dad on my own."

Aunt Larissa spoke up. "I'll go in with you, dear. Randy and I will."

Sandy didn't say any more about it. Greg emerged from the reposing room a minute later.

"You're finished?" Sandy asked.

"Yes. You can go in now." He held the door open slightly.

"But . . . but . . ." Sandy was aghast. "But did you have enough time?"

"I did what I needed to do."

Sandy, Larissa, and Randy went in to see his father's body while Greg wandered down the hallway.

The Lipman and Sons Funeral Home was very different from the ornate, spacious Hunt Chapel. This building felt squished but homey.

The staff had already prepared the reception room where his father's funeral service would be held the next day. Ten rows of sixteen chairs each were lined up perfectly, divided into left and right sections. Flower arrangements already stood at the front of the room with a portrait of Dad just off to the right. The only thing missing was the casket.

Beside the door was a wooden stand with a stack of printed papers on it. Greg pulled the top sheet off and read: *A Celebration of the Life of Lawrence Lucian Patterson*. The order of service followed.

He dropped the sheet back on top of the stack and reached the door of the reposing room just as Sandy, Randy, and Larissa were stepping out. Sandy was dabbing her eyes with a scrunched-up tissue.

"Can I talk to you in private for a moment?" Greg could hear his frustration coming through in his voice.

"Yes. Of course."

Greg led her toward the chapel entrance and the stand

with the papers on top. He slid the top one off again and held it up to her.

"I think maybe there's been a mistake in the order of service."

Sandy took the sheet and scanned it from top to bottom. "What do you mean? Everything's there."

He reached over and tapped his finger near the bottom of the list. "Words of remembrance? What's that about?"

"It's—it's a eulogy. A chance for you to share some memories of Dad."

"I don't remember discussing that."

"We didn't discuss it. I guess I didn't think we needed to."

He pulled the sheet out of her hands and laid it back on the stack. "According to that, I'm supposed to get up in front of everybody tomorrow and talk. Why wouldn't I want to know about it?"

She looked confused. "I thought you weren't afraid to speak in public. I just—"

"I'm not. That's not the issue."

"What is the issue?"

He shook his head sullenly. Sandy looked hurt. She entered the chapel and sat on the back row.

"I wasn't trying to be insensitive. Honestly! It never occurred to me that you wouldn't want to do it."

"Not everyone's grieving process is the same."

"I know."

He remembered a similar spat between them over the planning of Dad's seventieth-birthday party—Sandy rushing ahead with a grand vision while Greg balked in the background, trying to decide if the point was worth fighting over.

"What are we gonna do about it?"

"I don't know. I'm really sorry, Greg. I should've checked with you."

"Yeah." He said it simply, without indignation.

"I don't think we can change the programs. But maybe Pastor Fuller could skip over your part. I can talk to him."

"Thank you. It's not that I don't love Dad or have good memories of him. I just—" She looked at him curiously, and he hastened on. "You'll do a fantastic job with yours, I'm sure."

"Thanks. I'm just hoping to get through the whole thing without bursting into tears!"

Sandy's tears stopped her twice at the funeral the next morning as she shared memories of their dad. When she sat down afterward, she squeezed Greg's hand firmly and didn't let go.

At the podium, Pastor Fuller asked the crowd to join together in singing Larry's favorite hymn. Greg felt Sandy lean toward him.

"I forgot to talk to Pastor," she whispered, her eyes wide with sudden panic. "He doesn't know to skip your eulogy!"

Greg's stomach began to churn. Sandy mouthed an apology as the funeralgoers sang, "Yes, we'll gather at the river . . ."

It wasn't an issue of whether he could do it.

"The beautiful, the beautiful river."

He could share a quick story and sit back down.

"Gather with the saints at the river."

But he couldn't get past an overwhelming revulsion at the thought of it.

"That flows from the throne of God."

The organist sustained the last note of the song just long enough for Pastor Fuller to return to his seat. When he turned around and saw that Larry's son hadn't replaced him at the podium, he looked over at Greg with concern.

Greg remained rooted to his chair. He could feel the people around him realize that something was awry. Pastor sent a questioning look at Greg and discreetly motioned for him to take the stage.

Finally, Greg shook his head at Pastor Fuller and lowered his face into his hands. From several comments he received later, he understood that most people in the room thought he'd been overcome with emotion. The truth was, he sat there covering his face because it was all he could think of to do.

Pastor Fuller hurried to the front.

"It's never easy to say good-bye to someone we love. Even when we know we'll see that person again. As Christians, we don't grieve as those who have no hope, but that doesn't mean we don't grieve."

He continued the service, and Greg felt both relieved and conspicuous until the funeral was over.

Afterward, he lingered in the corner of the lobby while Sandy stood near the door of the chapel talking, hugging, crying, and laughing.

"Hi, Greg."

She had a rich, smooth speaking voice—especially when she talked on the phone or taught a class. When they first met, Greg teased Alicia about being "born to broadcast," but the profession had never interested her.

She was standing near the exterior door. Her hair, deep brown and straight, extended midway down her back, and her shimmering green eyes stood out in bright contrast.

"Alicia. You're here?"

"Sandy called me yesterday. She wanted to know if I needed a place to stay for your dad's funeral, but I had no idea what was going on. Why didn't you tell me, Greg?"

"I wasn't sure if . . ." he trailed off.

"You weren't sure I'd want to be here?" She spoke softly in the crowded lobby, but Greg could hear the indignation in her voice.

"I wasn't sure if you'd be able to make it."

"You didn't even try to find out."

Greg buried his hands in his pockets. "I didn't know if it would be weird for you."

"Weird for me? Regardless of whatever problems you and I have, he was—he is—my father-in-law. I loved him very much." She weighed her words before continuing. "Maybe you were afraid it would be weird for you."

She said it without malice, but to Greg it felt like a jab. He almost retorted sarcastically, but the pain he saw in her eyes held him in check.

"Is Summer here?"

"No. She wanted to come, but she had that big internship interview today."

"Oh yeah. That's right."

"If she'd been given a little more advance notice—more than a day—she might have been able to work something out. She almost canceled the interview, but I told her to stay. She's really upset."

"Yeah."

She no longer sounded angry. "What about you? Are you holding up OK?"

"It's been a whirlwind couple of days."

"I can imagine." They heard Sandy start sobbing again, and both looked toward the door of the chapel where she was being embraced by an older woman. "This is good for her," said Alicia. "To see all of these people here who loved your dad. The service was beautiful. Very fitting for such a kind soul."

Greg feared she would inquire about his failure to give his eulogy. But she didn't mention it.

Instead, she hugged him. "I'm so sorry, Greg. What an awful thing for you and Sandy. For all of us."

In the fifteen years since their separation, physical contact between them had been rare and stilted. But as she wrapped her arms around his chest in the funeral home lobby, Greg allowed himself to sink into her presence and her embrace.

"I'm sorry I didn't tell you about Dad. I was going to after I got back home."

She smoothed her hair back past her ears. "I wish you would trust me, Greg. And Summer. This was incredibly hurtful to us both."

He didn't stand next to her during the graveside service. She and Sandy linked arms on one side of the coffin while Greg stood a few yards apart. Pastor Fuller kept the proceedings short and simple, and the crowd of mourners dispersed. Most were headed to the church for a meal.

Greg resisted Sandy's pleas to join them.

"I think I'd prefer to be alone, if that's OK."

He knew she didn't understand. She couldn't. Every instinct in her soul pushed her closer to others to find connection and comfort in the midst of her pain. His urge to retreat utterly baffled her, but she didn't argue.

It was just after two o'clock. Greg drove around for a while, picking up a chicken sandwich from a drive-through. He parked in the shade of a tree and ate in silence as one word from his conversation with Alicia festered inside him.

Trust.

The shopping center contained a typical assortment of stores—shoes, vaping supplies, copy shop, pets, sushi. The pet store reminded Greg of the little girl looking for her rabbit. He knew the chances of her ever seeing Dipper again were almost nothing. The little guy's life likely ended in the jaws of some neighborhood predator roaming through the night.

Greg finished his sandwich and went into the pet store. He emerged fifteen minutes later with a cardboard box.

Back in his old neighborhood, he stopped in front of Dipper's house. Though this idea had begun as a whim, he strode up to the front door with a bounce in his step and a grin on his face.

A young man—the girl's father, no doubt—answered his knock.

"Can I help you?"

"Yes! I was just wondering if your daughter ever found her rabbit."

"Excuse me?" The man had opened the door only partway and was standing firmly between it and the doorframe.

"Oh! I'm sorry. I should explain. My name is Greg. I was here in the neighborhood yesterday afternoon, and I met your daughter. She was sitting there in the yard hoping to find her rabbit, Dipper."

"OK."

"I assumed she wouldn't find him, and . . ." He held up the box. "I just hate for her to have to deal with such a—"

"The rabbit came back."

"It did?" Greg was genuinely shocked.

"We think he was under the deck the whole time! He's back in his cage, safe and sound."

"Oh. That's fantastic!"

"Did you?" The man pointed to the box. "Did you buy her a new rabbit?"

"I just . . . felt badly for her. Thought maybe I could help."

"Do we know you? You live here in the neighborhood?"

"No, no! I don't. I used to, but . . ." Greg was flustered. "Anyway, I'm sorry to bother you. Please tell your daughter I'm glad she found him."

"What was your name?"

"Greg."

"OK. I'll tell her."

The man shut the door with an uncomfortable smile as Greg walked quickly toward his rental car. He stopped short of opening the door and looked over at his old house.

He remembered the day of his mother's funeral. It was also a Thursday. As the family filed out the front door of the house to go to the funeral home, Grandma cried out, "Oh, dear Lord! Now what? There's a run in my nylons!" She stopped on the crackled sidewalk (it had since been repaired) and stared at the small rip in the sheer fabric covering her left calf. She stood that way for a while before she crumpled to the front step, wailing. She ran her fingers across the rip over and over.

Dad rushed to her and put his arm around her shoulder. "Dorothy! Dorothy! It's OK. It's fine. We will get through this together. I promise. You won't be left alone. You'll never have to be alone!"

"Can I help you with something?"

Greg had wandered across the street and was standing on the edge of his old front lawn. The house's current resident was leaning around his screen door with a concerned look.

"Oh! No, sir. I used to live here, and I haven't seen the house in a while."

"I thought you were delivering a package." The man nodded at Greg's box.

"No, this isn't a delivery. Sorry to bother you." Greg scooted to the SUV and tried not to feel foolish as he drove back to the pet store to return the rabbit.

CHAPTER 10

*T*he next day, back-to-back flight delays kept Greg from touching down in Scranton until just before midnight. Even though he was home and in bed by one thirty, he didn't fall asleep until somewhere around three o'clock. He felt aimless and tired for most of Saturday, but on Sunday morning, his eyes popped open at eight. He flipped his blankets back and stumbled into the kitchen.

By midmorning, he stood in front of Starlight's door as she pulled it open with a flourish. "Come in! Come in!"

Ever since Summer's visit several weeks before, Greg had thought about his daughter's loaded questions every time he walked into Starlight's house. Today he and Starlight carried on their usual banter as Greg won several consecutive games of hearts. He was refilling his coffee at her kitchen counter when she caught him off guard.

"What's going on with you?"

"What do you mean?"

"You're not yourself today."

"Really?"

He felt anxious. Before leaving for Colorado, he'd insisted to Gladys that she tell no one about his whereabouts or the reason for his absence. It was unlikely that Starlight had somehow found out. Still, she pressed him.

"Yes. Something's going on. What is it?"

He avoided her gaze by stirring in some cream and sugar. "If there were something going on, who says I would tell you about it?"

He tried to sound lighthearted.

She shrugged. "Nobody says you *have* to tell me, Doc. I'm just curious by nature."

He returned to the table. "You know what they say about curiosity and the cat, don't you?"

"If you insist on maintaining this facade that everything's hunky-dory and all is well, then I guess we're done here. Have a nice week."

She said it in the way Greg had tried to speak a moment earlier, though she did a much better job of pulling it off— teasing, but just playful enough to keep from sounding like a jerk. He stared down at his coffee mug.

"Actually, the truth is I got some bad news this week."

Thinking of the moment later that night, Greg couldn't pinpoint why he felt the urge to open up to Starlight. She listened without a single interruption while he told her about Dad's accident, Sandy, the funeral. He even mentioned the bunny because he figured correctly that she'd enjoy that part of the story.

"So you really sat there and skipped your eulogy entirely?"

"Yup."

"That's bold! No one ever asked why you didn't say anything?"

"Nope. Most people thought I was too emotional to speak."

"Well, I don't blame you for skipping it."

This surprised him. "You don't?"

"I've always felt that eulogies are kind of creepy."

"I guess so."

"Maybe *creepy*'s not the right word. At the very least, they're dishonest. Nobody's as good in real life as they sound in a eulogy."

He relaxed slightly for the first time all week. They talked more, and Greg eventually told her about his conversation with Alicia. Starlight watched him closely as she listened.

"So how did it end?"

"The conversation?"

"The marriage."

He balked. "Oh."

"You've never talked much about it. Probably because it's none of my business!"

"No, it's OK. It's part of my life. No sense in ignoring it."

"So what happened?"

"Would you believe me if I said I don't know?"

"No."

"For starters, the marriage never ended—technically." He deliberated before proceeding. "But the truth is—I'm . . . I'm not an easy person to be with. I've got issues."

"Tell me one person who doesn't," she smirked.

"Good point." He leaned back in his chair and fished for a suitable answer. "Two people can approach life in drastically different ways and get through just fine. But there are times when certain things—certain moments—come along and those differences get too big to overcome. The gap gets too wide."

"I suppose that makes sense if you're explaining it to a ten-year-old."

"What?"

"Come on, Greg! That was such a canned answer. Are you really telling me that's all that happened between you two? The gap got too wide?"

She'd flustered him. He felt his face turning red. "I . . . I mean . . . yes. That's what I'm saying. If that's not it, then I really don't know!"

"I'll bet you do. Somewhere down deep. I'm not trying to sound like a butthead. I'm just surprised. All this time I figured there was some big blowup between you two."

"Neither of us are 'big blowup' kind of people." He owed her no further explanation but felt compelled to offer one anyway. "Who we are in our teens or our twenties—that's not us. I mean—it's not who we'll turn out to be. It can't be. Too little of life has gotten in the way by that point. But by the time we realize who we've become—the person life has turned us into—it's too late to do much about it, you know?"

"Jeez, I hope not."

"What?"

"If the person we are now is the best we can be, well, let's just say I'm screwed!"

He laughed. "I guess I am too!"

She smiled, and Greg could see she was backing away from her curiosity. "All else aside, I understand why you didn't tell her about your dad."

"Really?"

"I do. But I also understand why she got so pissed off at you."

"You're a confusing person."

She beamed. "Yes! I am. Take it or leave it, Doc. Take it or leave it."

That evening, with just a few minutes left on the forty-second day since Darren Horowitz's heart attack, the next drop finally pulled free from the old faucet.

The call came in while Greg was asleep in his recliner, a Western murmuring on the TV. He hit the power button on the remote as he answered his phone.

It was Gerry Wilson. Ernie had passed away in his bed about an hour before.

Greg thanked her for the call and stared at the blank TV

screen. He pictured the old man pouring orange juice on his roses to make sure he wasn't being poisoned by his wife. Though Greg found the image laughable, he couldn't muster a chuckle or even a smile. He felt sad and angry that he hadn't been able to see Ernie in the office recently. He clicked off the living-room light and went to bed.

CHAPTER 11

"*O*nly five left."

Ambrose looked irritated as he said these words. Allen, in the chair next to him, seemed distracted. Greg was behind his desk flicking a pen between his fingers.

The brothers had conducted Ernie Wilson's funeral the previous day. It had been a grand event with Gerry at its center, soaking up the attention eagerly yet as modestly as social convention required of a grieving wife. A string quartet from the Eastman School of Music provided the musical backdrop, and a Pennsylvania state senator headlined the eulogists. Word around the Hunt Chapel was that Gerry had tried to get a U.S. senator to attend, but was forced to settle for the lower-tier lawmaker. That afternoon, Ernie's casket was lowered into the ground in an area of Cotterman Cemetery that formerly belonged to Jacob Cohen's descendants.

"How many left on the list?"

"One hundred and nine."

Greg perked up. "Wow! You've had some people drop out."

"Yes, but we still have more than a hundred people too many." It was Allen. "And the ones who are still on the list are probably the most stubborn ones. You know, the real hard-core people who won't give up for anything!"

To Greg's relief, Gladys beeped in just then on the intercom and announced the arrival of his next patient. Greg sent the Wannamakers on their way through the lobby and ushered Opal Ridgley into the exam room.

"How are we feeling this afternoon?"

"I feel well, thank you." Opal was slender, with rusty red and gray hair pulled firmly away from her face into a short ponytail. She'd been a resident of Emmitsville for decades and one of Greg's most consistent patients for the last fifteen years.

"I'm not surprised to hear it. You're one of the healthiest people I know."

"Thank you." She motioned toward the hallway. "Was that the Wannamaker brothers I saw leaving just now?"

"Yes, ma'am, it was." Greg settled easily into his routine of chatting while examining his patient. He'd always preferred talking to people when he had doctoral duties to distract him from any awkward silences. "They swing by here every so often so I can commiserate with them."

Opal sat on the edge of the exam table, straight-backed and solemn faced. "About what?"

"You haven't heard? About the situation over at Cotterman Cemetery?"

"I've heard. I was at the meeting last month. I didn't realize that you were involved in it. Are you on the waiting list?"

Greg hadn't noticed her that night. "I'm not involved. Not officially anyway." He waited while her blood pressure registered on the dial. "I've been in the background trying to help them sort through it all. Sort of an advisor in residence, if you will. I'm definitely not on the waiting list."

"Why do you say it that way?"

"What way?"

"Dismissively. You're not interested in a Cotterman burial site?" Her voice was low-pitched and firm, making Greg feel uncomfortable.

"I'm not."

"Why is that?"

"Well . . ." He wheeled himself away from the exam table on his padded stool and held the ends of his stethoscope, which hung around his neck, with each hand. "I guess for starters I'm not planning on being buried anytime soon."

"Most people aren't."

"Yes. That shouldn't surprise me, considering my line of work." The conversation felt like it was beginning to turn hostile, and Greg wanted to find a way out of it quickly. "I'm a transplant to the valley. In some ways, I still feel like a newcomer. I know Cotterman is special to a lot of people around here, but honestly, it isn't to me."

"Fair enough. But certainly you can see how others might feel differently."

"Of course. But even if I was native to Emmitsville, I can't picture myself getting so worked up about a cemetery. I think it's—it's really kind of ridiculous. In the end, they're just six holes in the ground, right?" As soon as he said it, he wished he hadn't. She was tight-lipped and steely eyed.

"Five holes in the ground."

"Oh yeah. Five."

"That's a rather cynical perspective, wouldn't you say?"

Greg pulled her chart off the nearby countertop and jotted a few lines with his pen. "Realistic, I guess."

She stood and pulled her jacket on. "I agree with you on one point. The situation is ridiculous. This waiting list is . . . it's preposterous! To force all of us into this macabre scheme is offensive. I don't understand why they don't allow those who can afford it to buy a plot at a higher price. Those who can will pay up, and those who can't will just have to do without!"

Greg found a way to redirect the conversation toward her next appointment, and was relieved to see her out knowing she wouldn't return for six months. By then, he hoped the five spots would be filled and the excitement long gone.

He brought up his visit with Opal the following Sunday morning in Starlight's living room.

"I'm guessing she's one of those who can afford to pay a higher price for Cotterman?" Starlight wondered.

"I assume so."

"Sounds like you ruffled her feathers. Did you mention that the waiting list was your idea?" They were on the couch and she poked him playfully in the ribs.

"I was going to, but I never got around to it."

"How convenient. I think I agree with her about one thing, though."

"Really?"

"You are a bit cynical sometimes."

"What do you mean?"

"Oh, come on, Greg! I can hear it in your voice when you talk about this town. You're the most un-Emmitsvillian person in Emmitsville! I've heard it lately whenever you mention Cotterman. You've got some disdain stewing down there in your gut." She pointed to his midsection.

"I thought you agreed with me about that stuff. How many times have we poked fun at these people—trying to outdo their neighbors or get their name on a building?"

"Quite a few."

"So how are you any different than me?"

"I dunno. Maybe I'm not."

"You're confusing."

"Yup. You've mentioned that before." She smiled with satisfaction. "Hey, speaking of women that confuse you, how has your sister been since the funeral?"

"Uh—I haven't talked to her."

"Greg! Why not?"

"No particular reason. I just haven't."

"And what about Alicia? Is she still mad at you? I know it's none of my business, but I'm asking anyway."

Greg felt self-conscious whenever Alicia found her way into his conversations with Starlight. "Uh—I'm guessing she's cooled down."

"Haven't talked to her either, huh?"

"Nope. I did chat with Summer last week though. She's gotten over it . . . I think."

"She doesn't strike me as one to hold a grudge."

"Definitely not. She's a gracious soul. So kind."

Starlight popped into the kitchen to retrieve blueberry muffins from the oven. She returned with half a dozen on a small platter, steam radiating off the golden-brown bread and the sharp smell of berries filling the room.

"Getting back to your cynicism about Cotterman for a minute."

"Do we have to?"

"I think it's admirable that you've helped the Wannamakers despite your personal feelings about the futility of it all."

"Thanks, I think." Greg took a bite.

"Your idea about the waiting list was pretty good, but there's a better way to go about it that wouldn't tick off people like Opal Ridgely so much."

"Says who?"

"Says me."

She stood and crossed to her front window, pointing through it. "The Wannamakers don't have a space problem. They have a perception problem."

He joined her at the window to see where she was pointing. "Can you elaborate?"

"Everyone wants to be buried in Cotterman because, for some illogical reason, it's considered special. You and I are smart enough to know that it's full of worms and animal crap just like every other piece of land around here, but our neighbors don't see it that way. Their *perception* is different." Greg realized where she was pointing—in the direction of the cemetery. "Mr. Emmit Whoever-He-Was buried his kid there a hundred years ago, and from then on everyone wants a piece of the place."

"OK . . . ?"

"It means you and the Wannamakers need to figure out a way to change everyone's perception of Cotterman. If people don't perceive it the same way they do now, they won't worry so much about getting a spot in there!" She returned to the couch and plopped into the cushions.

"Figure out a way to change the perception." He was still standing in front of the window, but he turned toward her. "You say that like it's easy, but I don't think it is. You just pointed out there's a hundred years of history working against that."

"Yes, but that doesn't mean it's impossible."

"So, let's say we tried to do that. How would we?"

"The way I figure it, you—*they*—have two directions they could take it. On one hand, they could try to make Cotterman seem less desirable. It sits on a fault line or it's sopping in toxic waste. Something like that." Her eyes lit up, and she spoke enthusiastically. Greg realized she'd been thinking about this for a while.

"That'd be a tough sell. Everybody knows the land is pristine, and I don't think it would bother most people around here to violate Native American land."

"True. So, if you can't make Cotterman *less* desirable, then you could try to make some other option *more* desirable."

"As in?"

"As in coming up with some alternate idea that is so amazing that anyone who sticks with Cotterman seems like an idiot!"

Greg returned to the armchair. "Put their one-upmanship

to use and whittle away the waiting list at the same time. Interesting theory."

"Anyway, there it is. You guys have been going about it all wrong. Eventually you'll come to see that I'm right."

"You keep lumping me in with them. Who says I'll even give it a second thought? I've offered my two cents to Ambrose and Allen already. That's all I got." He pulled the fabric of one pocket inside out to demonstrate.

"Oh, you've got more to give. I have no doubt that you do."

"How can you be so sure?"

"Because I know that you love to solve puzzles. Underneath all of the posturing and prestige, this cemetery situation is nothing more than a big puzzle waiting to be solved—by someone just like you!"

CHAPTER 12

*G*reg was eating an early lunch in the Blue Dot Diner on the Wednesday after Thanksgiving when Archie Early plopped down opposite him in the booth.

"Howdy, Doc! Looks like you had yourself a fine lunch there." Archie pointed at the remnants on Greg's plate. "Lemme guess. Grilled cheese and tomato soup?"

"One of my favorites."

"So I heard some news just now."

"Is that so?"

"Alec Ruttiger fell into the Grand Canyon yesterday. He's dead."

Greg nearly choked on a last spoonful of soup. "You're kidding!"

"Nope. True as gospel. Apparently he was out there on some sort of hiking-camping trip. I gotta say, I admire that. He's older than me! Well, he was until yesterday."

"What happened?"

"Not sure exactly. Musta slipped or something of that nature. They say he was already gone by the time rescue workers got to him. Took 'em nearly an hour to get down there."

"That's horrible."

"It is. I mean, it's not like Alec and me were close friends, but we were both single men in this town who enjoyed the company of the ladies every now and again so I guess you could say we circled in each other's orbits. It's a shame he's gone."

"I'm not sure a lot of folks will agree with you on that."

Archie considered this briefly. "I reckon you're right. Alec was much better at making enemies than friends. Still, he's got his place in Cotterman."

Alec's body didn't arrive from Arizona until the following week, and the details of his final arrangements became public several days after that. Alec had been unmarried at the time of his death, and any remaining relatives were a mystery to most of the town. It was Ambrose who announced that the funeral service would be held on a Friday afternoon.

Greg arrived early and sat near the back of the Hunt Chapel listening to snippets of conversation from those filling in the seats around him.

"I heard he was posing for a picture on the edge of the canyon where there wasn't a railing. He was looking at the cameraman and he stepped too far back. Slipped and fell right off!"

"That's horrible. How far did he fall?"

"Several hundred feet at least."

"What an awful way to go."

"Humph. Probably a good thing he didn't make it. The weasel would've tried to sue the National Park Service or the U.S. government for negligence. Do you know he once took a young family to court after he hit their car with his Mercedes?"

"You're joking!"

"Not a bit. He sued them for damages because the bicycle rack on the back of their minivan crashed through his window when he hit them. He argued they were being reckless by keeping the rack on their van when it wasn't in use! The accident was *his* fault, but he sued them. Can you believe that?"

Knowing Alec's tenacity and lack of scruples, Greg assumed he won the lawsuit.

When Ambrose walked up to the podium to begin the service, the room was slightly more than half full. But the area around Ambrose at the front of the chapel was empty. There were no casket, no flowers, and no indication that a funeral was taking place.

"Good afternoon. Welcome to the funeral service for Alec Ruttiger. I've been asked to officiate today's proceedings, and —and so that's what I'm doing." Greg noticed that Ambrose seemed uncomfortable, even hesitant. He held a sheet of paper in his hands.

"Alec has requested that no one offer any eulogies or readings today. He also asked that no flowers be displayed. Essentially, today's service will consist of just two parts—a video and a song. As so many of you know, my brother and I pride ourselves on honoring our customers' final wishes as best we can. So with that, we will begin."

The house lights dimmed and the projection screen unrolled from the ceiling. When the screen lit up, the funeralgoers saw Alec Ruttiger in a leather recliner, sneering at them.

"Well, hello, my fellow citizens of Emmitsville!" Alec's gravelly voice pounded through the chapel's sound system. "Bet you weren't expecting this, now were ya?" He grinned at the camera as if waiting for someone in the audience to respond. "In case you're wondering, let me just go ahead and spell it out for you. Yes, this is one of those *if you're watching this then that means I'm dead* sort of things. It's a bit cliché, I know, but . . . oh, well! It's the best I could come up with.

"Now, there's a couple of things I want to clear up right away so that there's no confusion or complaints over what's about to happen. I know most of you pretty well, and I wouldn't put it past some of you to try and steal my thunder from me somehow. Don't even think about it! I've put this whole thing together and it's ironclad. Trust me. I'm a lawyer and a pretty damn good one at that."

Greg turned toward the back corner of the chapel. The glow of the projection screen lit up Ambrose and Allen, standing side by side in their dark suits and crimson ties. Greg could see deeply etched frowns on their faces.

"First off, you need to know that I'm filming this clip on October 13. If that date doesn't mean anything to you, let me give you a quick reminder. Last week we had a town meeting right there in Hunt Chapel about Cotterman Cemetery, and it looks like only a few lucky stiffs will actually get to be buried on the hillside. Everyone else is just . . . screwed, I guess.

"Second, I want to be clear that I am on the waiting list for Cotterman. Yup! I haven't been in town as long as most of you, but I signed up right away. Got a letter from the funeral home right here." He held up a sheet of tan parchment paper.

"Third, I want to go on record with this. I have no idea who's gonna get those last six spots. Of course I don't! How could I? I'm just a mere mortal suffering at the cruel hands of fate like all the rest of you schmucks. I've got no inside track on this thing. I'm doing all of this on a whim. For all I know, I might live another thirty years. If that happens, then this video will waste away never to be seen.

"But I'm guessing that's not the case. Call it a hunch or some extraterrestrial premonition or something like that, but I got this feeling I'm gonna be one of the chosen six. If so, I've made my final wishes very clear. It's all in writing. Notarized. The whole nine yards. Ambrose and Allen Wannamaker don't know about it yet, but they will if and when the time comes. I've made damn well sure of that!

"So this is how it's all going down, folks. If I kick off in time to get one of those six spots, I'm not gonna be buried in my space. You heard that right. I'm taking my spot, but I'm not using it for me. I'm using it for this guy." Alec held up a framed picture of a German shepherd. "This is Rickles. I had him with me for nearly fifteen years. One hell of a dog, let me tell ya. He outlasted two wives and half a dozen flings! He was a lot nicer to be around than most of them, too. A lot less whining, that's for sure. The sweet old fellow finally died a couple of months ago. Just got too old, I think." Alec looked at the picture admiringly.

"I had him cremated, and his ashes have been sitting in my house ever since. I hadn't really known what to do with them. Until a few days ago. It occurred to me that ol' Rickles should get a place up there in Cotterman. He deserves it a lot more than most of us—including me. He was good . . . and kind . . . and way less annoying than most of you.

"Now, I know what you're thinking. *He can't do that, can he?* Let me give you the short answer. I sure can! I've checked it all out. As long as the animal's body has been disposed of legally—in this case through 'incineration in accordance with regulations governing air quality'—and as long as the cemetery itself has no policies against it (they don't, I checked), then there's nothing stopping me from giving my burial plot to my best friend Rickles. And that's exactly what I plan to do!"

He paused for another obnoxious grin. Whispers across the room had begun shortly after the video started and were increasing as Alec droned on.

"If any of you are wondering what's gonna happen to me—to my remains, that is—don't worry a bit. They're gonna incinerate me 'in accordance with regulations governing air quality,' and that will be the end of that. I'll be honest with you. This isn't what I was planning when I first set up an estate plan. But now that I see the way things are playing out? I think I like this a lot better. Like I said, I'm just doing it on a whim, and my plan might come to nothing. Then again, maybe it won't. Either way, I'm getting one hell of a kick out of it all. I haven't had this much fun in years!"

The screen went dark.

As the lights faded up, Ambrose trudged back to the podium. He looked distraught before the stunned and now silent audience.

"That concludes this funeral service. As you leave today, Mr. Ruttiger has requested that we play a song. Thank you for being here."

As "Another One Bites the Dust" played over the speakers, Greg didn't wait around to listen to the conversations surrounding him. He headed straight for the double doors. In the lobby he circled around the corner to the long hallway running parallel to the chapel. A few moments later, Ambrose burst through the door from the chapel to the hallway, slamming it behind him. He didn't at first notice Greg standing to his left.

"Are you OK?" Greg ventured.

Ambrose looked up in alarm, but relaxed when he saw Greg.

"Not really."

"That was—wow! I was not expecting that."

"I don't think anyone was."

"It's probably the shortest funeral I've ever been to."

"No doubt."

"Can he really put his dog's ashes up there?"

Ambrose loosened his tie and leaned against the wall. "Yes. He can. It's like he said on the video. There's no law against it, and we don't have any policy here against it. That is—we *haven't* had one. You can be sure Allen and I are going to change that straightaway!"

"Did you have to follow all his instructions exactly?"

Ambrose seemed offended by the question. "Greg. We are bound to meet our customers' needs and requests. That's part of the business. It's not our job to judge."

"What about the video? That riled you the most, didn't it?"

"For sure."

"Couldn't you have just skipped it and done the dog thing in secret? No one else would ever be the wiser. Certainly not Alec."

"It—it was a part of his final wishes. He wanted everyone to see it. As much as I hated to play it, it was my responsibility to give him what he wanted. Out of respect for the dead."

"Interesting."

Ambrose stood up straight and fumed. "It's not interesting, Greg. It's sickening. It's crude." He sputtered as he struggled to speak his mind. "Alec . . . the man was an obnoxious loudmouth! Better off at the bottom of the Grand Canyon."

"Ambrose!" Greg was taken back by the funeral director's fierceness. "I've never seen you like this. So much for respecting the dead, huh?"

"I apologize for the outburst. I know it's not very professional of me, but . . . but you don't really mind."

Greg chuckled. "No. I don't mind. I agree. It was an obnoxious thing for Alec to do. I guess if there's any silver lining here it's that you're almost done with this mess."

"What do you mean?"

"It's another burial plot used up. Only four left. My guess is that a few more people will give up and take their names off the list."

Ambrose considered this. "You're probably right. Four more to go. Then . . ."

"Then what?"

"Then we get back to normal."

Alec's unconventional funeral reverberated throughout the town—especially among the hundred or so who were still on the waiting list. The loss of another burial plot in such a particularly spiteful manner seemed to raise the stakes for those still hoping for a place. Greg began to hear of various attempts to work around the system.

Gladys was the first to mention it.

"Some folks are trying to bribe others into taking their name off the list."

"You're kidding."

"Nope. I've heard of at least half a dozen people who've been offered some sort of bribe to give up. There's even been some threats of blackmail."

"That's gotta be made up!"

Gladys insisted. "Nope."

"What kind of blackmail?"

"Greg, a lot of these folks have known each other since they were kids in boarding school together. They've got a lifetime of secrets at their disposal. I'll bet some of those secrets are pretty dark and juicy."

"Is it working?"

"You tell me. You're the one in cahoots with the Wannamakers. What's the list look like these days?"

"I'm not in cahoots—whatever that means! But I do know the list is shrinking a little. Still a lot of people on it, though."

Days later Ambrose reported to Greg that he and Allen were regularly receiving offers of large sums of money to nix the waiting list and sell the plots directly.

"Is Opal Ridgely one of the people trying to buy you out?" asked Greg, recalling his confrontation with her in his office.

"Greg! I can't tell you that. The offers were made in confidence. Besides, I don't want to dignify them with any inkling of legitimacy."

"So, I take it you're not selling out."

"Of course not! Our reputation as a funeral home would be demolished."

Though Greg understood the brothers' resistance to the cash offers, he didn't at first agree with their refusal. They were well within their rights as businessmen to sell the plots to the highest bidders. It wasn't until one of his patients cornered him at the end of an examination and offered her own proposition that Greg realized how it must have made the Wannamakers feel.

"I've heard you're in with the brothers at the cemetery. You think maybe you can convince them to swing things my way? I could make it worth your while."

The initial shock Greg felt soon transformed into irritation and offense. *Just what kind of person does she think I am? Convince them to swing it her way? Do I look like some dirty politician?*

"I'm sorry. I can't do that."

He received two more similar offers in the following days —one in person and one over the phone.

From the first time Ambrose had taken him through the details of the situation four months earlier, Greg had always looked at the scenario with a mixture of amusement and scorn. It was all foolishness, but it was *their* foolishness. Let 'em eat their cake if they wanted it so badly.

Now he was starting to feel far less lighthearted about it all. The canceled doctor appointments. The obnoxious video. The bribes and blackmail.

He told Gladys he was taking an extra-long lunch. Emerging from his car at Lerner Park with a takeout bag from the Blue Dot, he found himself mulling over what Starlight had said a few weeks before. "Change the perception," Greg muttered as he strolled along the sidewalk on the west side of the park. "She's probably right, but how to do that for people whose sense of value is so warped and unrealistic?"

He sat on one of dozens of park benches along the sidewalks edging the large lawn area.

It's like trying to buy a Christmas gift for the person who already has everything except a yacht and a Rolex! he mused.

It was early January, and the bare branches in the frosty

sunlight were stark reminders to Greg that his least favorite season of the year would be hanging around for at least another month.

The horn of a blue BMW nearby began blaring as the car's owner fidgeted with a key fob.

If you're gonna spend the money to buy the thing, you might want to make sure you know how to operate it, buddy, Greg groused to himself. He didn't know the elderly man who eventually disabled the alarm and pulled the driver's-side door open, but he scowled from a distance. *It's probably got way more horsepower than you need, anyway.*

Just beyond the BMW, on the other side of Second Street, stood the Betty Cochran Memorial Library. Greg visited the library often but had never before wondered, *Who the heck is Betty Cochran and why is the library named after her?*

Nearly every public building or place of business in Emmitsville had the name of some deceased resident attached to it. Banks. The post office. Even the water-treatment plant. The park where Greg was sitting had been named after Albert Lerner, a wildly popular mayor who served several terms during Emmitsville's heyday in the 1920s. In most cases the namesake received the honor because they had donated enough money to the right people or pulled the right strings at the right time.

People in Emmitsville rarely spoke of or even knew anything about those whose names were engraved across the valley. Betty Cochran wasn't the only name Greg didn't recognize.

Summer would contend that their faded memory was beside the point. They died believing their legacy would live on.

Just one way of helping them "cope with oblivion," right?

He was staring at the library, which had recently installed a high-tech, full-color digital sign out front to replace the worn wooden placard from decades earlier. The screen displayed the library's name and a rotation of announcements for upcoming events.

Betty Cochran Memorial Library.

Summer's point of view began to resonate with him in a different way when he considered it in light of Starlight's opinion about the cemetery.

It's all about perception.

The images on the screen flashed and moved in brilliant arrays of color, but to Greg they signified something much different.

He was fairly certain he'd stumbled upon a solution to the Cotterman puzzle.

CHAPTER 13

*I*n the small meeting room adjacent to the Hunt Chapel, Ambrose, Allen, and Greg sat around the oval conference table in suit coats and ties. "I still can't picture Dad doing anything like this when he was running the place," said Ambrose, who had been in a foul mood all morning.

Allen interjected quietly. "It's the best idea anyone's had since this whole mess began."

They all looked through the room's only window, which faced the parking lot. A long white luxury sedan rolled up and parked.

"Allen, let's go." Ambrose motioned for his brother to follow him out of the room. A few minutes later they reentered with a man in a blue blazer and a woman in a white sun hat.

Greg stood up with what he hoped was a reassuring smile. "Mr. and Mrs. Risedale. It's good to see you!"

The woman sat without speaking, and the man muttered as he bent his knees painfully to drop into a chair. "Well, we're quite curious to hear what you're up to."

"Oh, I can assure you that we're not 'up to' anything, Mr. Risedale," said Ambrose. He smoothed out the lapels of his jacket and smiled. "We'll try not to take too much of your time this morning."

Mr. Risedale grunted. His wife muttered with pursed lips, "I've heard about all this. Some sort of computer program or something, right?"

Ambrose answered, "Maybe it will be best if I start from the beginning."

The Risedales waited for him to continue.

"I want to start by saying how sorry I am that we've reached this unusual situation with Cotterman Cemetery. You've both been respected citizens of Emmitsville for as long as I can remember. If it were up to me—well, me and my brother—we'd provide funeral services and burial plots to anyone and everyone who wants them. Unfortunately, we just don't have the ability to do that."

He spoke smoothly and sincerely. Greg was impressed, and the Risedales relaxed a bit.

Mr. Risedale said, "I remember when you were just little guys out in the cemetery raking leaves. Helping your father out. He was a great man, your father. I knew him well. He was a respectable businessman who did an outstanding job of taking care of this place." Greg watched Ambrose closely. The words appeared to land on the funeral director heavily.

"Yes, sir. I agree. My father was a wonderful person. I'm thankful for the example he set for us over the years in how he operated the funeral home and cemetery. Along those lines, I'm happy to tell you that we've created an option that will still allow you to be a part of the great heritage this place holds in our town."

Mrs. Risedale spoke sternly. "OK. Let's hear it."

Ambrose pulled a large sheet of paper from an envelope and unfolded it. "We're giving all of our clients—that is, those that are on the waiting list—the right of first refusal for an expansion we're planning right here in the funeral home."

"You're burying people inside the funeral home?"

"Not exactly." Ambrose slid the paper toward the couple and indicated the plans printed on it. "We're planning to turn the hallway just outside this room into a one-of-a-kind memorial display. There's an exciting new technology available that will allow us to display a three-dimensional image of each client on a high-definition screen. This image will feature the client's shoulders and head—similar to a bust you might see in a museum or art gallery. Only in this case, the bust will be digital and nearly lifelike."

Mr. Risedale was confused. "A . . . screen?"

"Yes, sir! It will be computer generated in incredibly high resolution. The image can be rotated around, 360 degrees. It can even speak to visitors when they are standing in front of the display."

Ambrose gestured toward the professional renderings on the sheet. "Our plan is to mount each screen on top of a pedestal approximately four feet tall. Clients will have the option of either a wooden or granite pedestal. Their name, date of birth, and date of death will be engraved on a plaque along with any other details the client might wish to include. As you can see on the schematic, the hallway affords us the space to provide nearly eighty clients with this unique opportunity."

"But . . . but what about the . . . remains?"

"Each pedestal will include space directly below the screen where an urn or something of the sort can be displayed."

Mrs. Risedale gasped. "Urn? You mean cremation?"

"Yes, ma'am."

"But no one gets cremated," she sputtered. "Here in Emmitsville, I mean."

"That's not completely accurate. It's not very common, but we do—"

"Of course it's not!" She was getting more agitated, while her husband's frown sank deeper into his face. "It's no wonder! Cremation is grotesque and, to be honest, I don't think it's very Christian-like."

"I don't really know about that, Mrs. Risedale."

Mr. Risedale jumped in. "So let me be clear about this. About your *plan*—although it sounds more like a two-bit scheme." Ambrose glanced sidewards at Greg. "Instead of a traditional burial in the cemetery, you want to turn us into some sort of computer program, stick us in a back hallway, and wait for us to talk to anyone who happens to pass by? That's your solution?"

Ambrose looked stricken. "I—um—I don't think that's accurate. The way you're characterizing it isn't at all what we're envisioning. I—I'm not describing it well enough."

"How could you possibly describe it well enough?" countered Mrs. Risedale. "It's a second-rate, sloppy solution, and you'll have a tough time convincing me otherwise."

Mr. Risedale added, "You said if it were up to you, you'd give a funeral service and burial plot to anyone who wanted it. Well, it is up to you! You're in charge here, and we want a traditional service and burial. So why don't you just sell us one right now. We're ready to pay whatever it takes!" The old man pulled out a checkbook and a pen.

"I—I can't do that. I'm sorry, but I just can't."

The Risedales stared angrily across the table. Ambrose pulled the paper timidly back while Allen kept his eyes low and his lips tight. Finally Greg said, "Mr. and Mrs. Risedale? Would you wait here for just a minute? I understand that you're upset, and I want a quick word with Allen and Ambrose."

In the hallway, Greg pulled the conference-room door shut behind them. "So, what's the plan?" asked Ambrose.

"Plan?"

"You told the Risedales—"

"You were about to crash and burn. I was trying to buy

you some time." Greg nodded at the door. "Mission accomplished."

"But what do we do now?"

"I have no idea. They don't seem to be buying into this."

Ambrose faced Greg. "I don't want to sound unkind, but this plan—this *scheme*—with the screens and the pedestals was *your* idea! Just like the waiting list. You put it together even though I've been uncomfortable with it from the beginning. I told you I didn't have a good feeling about it."

"I know, but—"

"If you hadn't talked us into it, I never would have come up with something so—so—unorthodox, and I would never have made such a fool of myself in front of people like the Risedales." Greg tried to interject again but Ambrose didn't miss a beat. "They're furious over your idea, and I think you should be the one to talk to them when we go back in."

"What am I going to say? I'm just here for moral support, remember? They've already told us they won't go for it."

Ambrose wilted. "I don't know. I don't know what any of us can do. Maybe we just forget the screens and let the waiting list run its course."

The silent seconds stretched into a minute. Eventually Ambrose asked, "Greg, will you please try to convince them to take our offer?"

"But you don't even like the idea."

"Right now it's the only one we have." Regret and fear brimmed in Ambrose's eyes as he pleaded, "My father trusted us to continue his legacy. This—all of this with the burial plots and the list and the bribes and the pressure— could ruin all of that. I'm not sure how much longer we can put up with it all."

Greg put a hand on Ambrose's shoulder. "It won't go on forever, Ambrose. It can't."

"I know, but that doesn't change anything for us in the present." Ambrose looked over his shoulder at the conference-room door. "I can't talk to them anymore. I messed everything up earlier. I think the plan has potential, but I'm not doing a good job of selling it. I've never been a good salesman. Never had to be. All of the cemetery plots were already sold by the time we came around."

"I'm no salesman either," said Greg. "Doesn't come up often in my line of work."

"You're better at talking to people than either of us."

"He's right," said Allen.

"Please, Greg."

He'd spent two weeks working out the details of the idea before convincing the brothers to opt in. It had been exciting to envision all of it with them. In his enthusiasm, he hadn't given much thought to the possibility that others might not see it favorably.

"Give me five minutes, and I'll come talk to them." He headed down the hall.

"Where are you going?"

"Outside. To think of what I'm going to say."

Standing on the front sidewalk, Greg allowed the cool winter wind to sweep past him while he considered his options. Though he wanted to leave, he knew that he wouldn't. Ambrose had touched the right nerve. It was *his* idea, and he was invested in seeing it succeed.

When he returned to the conference room, the atmosphere was as tense as when he'd left it, though—to their credit—the Risedales hadn't yet stormed out. Greg sat back down in his chair and summoned a compassionate smile.

"Mr. and Mrs. Risedale, thank you for waiting. I'm not sure what Ambrose told you while I was out, but—"

"He asked us to wait for you, and hasn't said a word since," Mrs. Risedale announced.

Greg leaned forward. "If it's all right, I'd like to say something before you make up your mind."

"We're listening."

"I said earlier that I could tell you're upset about all this."

"Darn right, we're upset! This whole meeting has been rather insulting."

"But you're not just angry." Greg tried to swallow his nervousness before continuing. "You're afraid."

Mrs. Risedale's eyebrows rose, but her husband was the one who spoke. "Excuse me?"

"I mean no disrespect when I say this, but I believe both of you are afraid. That's why you're here today."

"What could you possibly be referring to? Afraid?"

Greg nodded. "Yes. Let's not forget what all of the fuss is about. A cemetery. Burial plots. HD screens. We're not talking about a vacation rental that's been double-booked or a waiting list for a table at your favorite restaurant. The only reason we're having this discussion is that both of you are going to die someday."

Greg thought he heard a gasp from someone in the room, but he didn't break eye contact with the Risedales.

"I'm not trying to be disrespectful or unkind. I'm just stating a fact."

Mr. Risedale said, "It's true. But we're not afraid."

"But, you see, the thing is, I think you are. I think most people are afraid to die. Even if just a little. I've been a doctor half my life. I've seen it in the eyes of hundreds of people over the years. Doesn't matter if they're in the hospital bed or standing next to it. It's almost always there."

"What is?" asked Mrs. Risedale, her interest piqued.

"Fear. I mean, let's be honest. Nobody likes the idea of leaving this life—especially when we don't really know what's on the other side of it."

"So what's your point? You're going to preach a sermon now?"

"No! Nothing of the sort," Greg chuckled. "I just want you to think carefully about all of this. About your decision. Part of the reason you want to be buried in Cotterman is that it makes you feel better about not being here . . . alive. Some might say it's a way of coping with oblivion. The location. The town's history. Your headstone. Most of it just comes down to making you feel better."

Their expressions were difficult to interpret, so Greg pressed on. "I'm not saying that's a bad thing. I suppose it's just a natural human response. But are you telling us that the only possible way for you to feel better about passing on is to get one of those last few spots? You're hanging all of your hopes on that?"

"Not necessarily."

"Ambrose and Allen are giving you the opportunity—the *first* opportunity—to be a part of something different and special. These pedestals. The screens. This will be truly unique. Don't think of it as just a hallway. Think of it as a hall of fame. An Emmitsville hall of fame.

"And it's not a back hallway like you said earlier. It's a prominent part of this great building. You walked down the hall to get to this meeting today. Think of all the visitors who will walk through it as they arrive for similar meetings for years to come. And what about funerals in the chapel? I have no doubt that many people will filter into the hallway before or after the service—especially when there is something significant here to see. Can't you picture it?"

Mrs. Risedale turned to gaze out the window. Her husband seemed to stare past Greg straight through the walls of the small conference room.

"I suppose so," Mr. Risedale said.

"Do you have grandchildren?"

"Yes. And great-grandchildren. Thirteen of them."

"Imagine your great-grandchildren having the chance to come to the hall of fame and see your image in lifelike 3-D! Like Ambrose said, you can even have the image speak to them."

"But what on earth would we say?"

"You can say whatever you want. It's all recorded ahead of time. You can tell them how much you love them. How proud you are of them. You can share wisdom for life. Whatever you want! Think about that. We're giving you the chance to let your image and your voice live on even though you're gone.

"Of course, you can keep your name on the waiting list and see what happens. It's obvious that a traditional burial is quite important to you. But let's be honest. That may or may not work out in the end. It's a risk. A gamble. The hall of fame carries no such risk. You will secure your spot the moment you sign on, and no one can ever take it away from you. What do you think?"

Neither Risedale answered; Greg wondered if he'd upset them even further. Their faces were still hardened and unsmiling.

Then Mrs. Risedale spoke up. "Thank you for all this, but I'm afraid that—"

"I think we should think it over." Mr. Risedale had turned in his chair to face his wife.

"You—you do?"

"Yes."

She was surprised by her husband's interruption, searching his eyes for a cue of some sort.

"Well, then. I guess we will think it over."

Mr. Risedale stood up. "If we decide to go with this idea, we should . . . ?"

"Just let us know," said Ambrose. "We have the paper work ready for signing!" He stood, extending his hand.

"All right. We'll let you know. But don't take our name off that waiting list just yet."

"No. No, sir. We definitely won't. Not till we hear from you directly."

Greg and the Wannamakers had only a few minutes to

relish their small victory. Their next appointment was arriving shortly.

"Greg, can you do it again?" Ambrose's mood had improved. "Give the pitch. Sell the idea."

Greg's impulse was to hand the reins back to the brothers, but this vanished as quickly as it appeared. They had some momentum, and he didn't see any sense in squandering it.

By the end of the day, the O'Conners had also agreed to consider places in the hall of fame, as had the Thompsons. The Brighams gave a flat refusal. It was during the first meeting of the afternoon that Greg, Ambrose, and Allen earned their first yes. Leroy Hastings pulled himself out of the running for Cotterman and filled out the paperwork for a spot in the hallway.

Greg went to bed that night with five maybes, three nos, three yeses, and a pestering sense of guilt over the knowledge that he didn't fully believe in what he'd been saying and selling to his fellow townsfolk all day.

CHAPTER 14

"When do you think we'll see the first pedestal and screen go in?"

On the first Sunday in February, Greg and Starlight sat in her kitchen with steaming mugs of tea.

"Over thirty people have bought in already. Chances are getting better every day."

"Boy, I can't wait to see one of them!"

"Really?"

"Sure. Why not? Why would I pass up the chance to see the digital disembodied head of one of my neighbors floating above their ashes?"

"Well, when you put it that way, who could resist?"

"Looks like my big idea was a good one!"

"Your idea?" Greg twirled a spoon in his tea as he waited for it to cool.

"I gave you the seed. You watered and grew it from there. Now the waiting list is almost down to a manageable number and the Wannamakers' business is booming. Thanks to me!" She winked at him. "And to some extent—you."

"To be fair, I think some of the credit for shrinking the list goes to Ernie Wilson, Alec Ruttiger, and Doreen Wolenski."

"Why do they get credit?"

"The pedestal plan is good, but part of the reason so many have dropped out from Cotterman is that there's so few spots left. Wouldn't you say?"

"I suppose so. The odds of getting in at this point aren't great."

"And they get worse every time another wait-lister dies." He tested his tea and found it was still too hot. "Even at the beginning, you had a better chance of winning a scratch game than getting buried in Cotterman."

"That's probably true, but the ones who are still holding on are *really* holding on."

"Thanks to Jane Lerner, no doubt."

Jane, who'd raised the ire of Alec Ruttiger at the town meeting last fall, had become somewhat of a cautionary tale to those on the waiting list. She'd rejected Greg's pitch for a pedestal several weeks before, still hoping to get into Cotterman. When Doreen Wolenski died a few days later and took another spot, Jane grew despondent. She contacted the Wannamakers about removing her name, only to choke on a grape at home that evening.

Starlight shook her head in amazement. "She missed it by four hours. Now, she's stuck out in Woodland Acres."

"I hope the whole thing is over soon. Cotterman all filled up and everyone moving on to other ridiculous obsessions."

"You realize you're hoping people will die, don't you? That's the only way for it to end."

Greg shrugged. "It's the way everything ends, isn't it?"

"Doctor!" She spoke with a shocked tone that sounded put on, though he wasn't entirely sure it was. "I've never heard you talk so flippantly about death!"

"Not flippant. I'm just . . . realistic."

They sipped and stared past each other into their own thoughts.

"This is pretty pathetic," said Starlight.

"What is?"

"It's Super Bowl Sunday. Most of the world is getting ready to watch TV and pig out on snacks, and we are sitting here in my kitchen like a pair of . . . monks. Or losers. I can't decide which."

"You want to go on vacation?"

Starlight mimicked surprise. "Dr. Greg! Are you asking me to go on vacation with you?"

He rushed to correct himself even as his heart fluttered a little. "No. No! I meant do *you* want to go on a vacation—for yourself. By yourself."

"Oh. I see."

"Why do you do that?"

"Do what?"

"Turn my words around on me."

She shrugged. "Defense mechanism, I suppose."

They speculated about what the next few months might bring to Emmitsville's little valley in the woods. All the while, Greg watched her eyes carefully and considered possible answers to the question he really wanted to ask.

Defense mechanism against what?

Later that month, Leland Potts died, giving the Wannamakers the opportunity to install him as the first member of the hall of fame.

The Hunt Chapel was nearly full for the memorial service, to the delight of Leland's family. The high attendance did, however, create a problem when the service was over and the time came for Leland's pedestal and screen to be unveiled. Bottlenecking in the hallway allowed only a few dozen people to witness the moment. The attendees who didn't leave altogether had to wait in the chapel for their chance to see the display.

"There's really nothing we can do about it," Ambrose muttered to Greg, hearing the disgruntled murmurs in the crowd.

Leland's pastor read some Scripture and offered a short

prayer before Ambrose pulled away the silver satin sheet, revealing the assemblage beneath.

The polished cherrywood pedestal stood waist-high with an engraved plaque shimmering near the top. Just below the plaque was a small, inset shelf, the final resting place for Leland's ashes—which had been emptied into a brandy snifter. Later, after the crowd was gone, one of the Wannamakers would swing closed the tiny window and lock the ashes in permanently.

Secured to the wall just above the pedestal was the oblong display screen, oriented vertically, like a portrait. The screen's casing and wires were hidden by a cherrywood frame.

As soon as Ambrose pulled the satin sheet away, the funeralgoers gasped. A high-resolution rendering of Leland smiled and blinked at them from the screen.

"It looks just like him!"

"That's amazing."

"It's almost too lifelike."

Leland's widow hobbled forward and brushed her bony index finger across the corner of the screen. Airy violin music began to play as a narrator recounted the highlights of Leland's life in a baritone voice. A slide show of pictures scrolled past. Finally, Leland's digital bust reappeared and began speaking to his unseen audience.

"My name is Leland Potts, and this is my legacy . . ." He spoke about his family and friends for nearly two minutes.

Greg observed from the far end of the hall. Everyone's eyes were fixed on the screen; they looked entranced by the images and sounds. For half an hour after the service, he tried to count the number of people who filed past, many tapping the screen to watch the presentation for themselves.

Change the perception, he thought. *It actually worked!*

The moment of seeing the pedestal for themselves was a tipping point for several more townsfolk—both wait-listers and otherwise. As spring arrived, the hall of fame was nearly sold out and the waiting list was down to less than twenty names.

On the day in mid-April when they sold the last available space in the hallway, the Wannamakers asked Greg to stop by their office and celebrate.

"I honestly never thought this idea would work, but you pulled it off, Greg." Ambrose looked more relaxed than he had in months.

"It was a team effort."

"Thanks to the momentum you built up. Once people caught the vision, the pedestals basically sold themselves."

There were times when Greg still felt uncomfortable with the hall-of-fame idea and the pitch he'd used to sell it. Others walked the hallway marveling at the legacies it would hold, but Greg found the sight strange and off-putting. He kept this to himself.

"So the hallway is all booked up. How's the waiting list?"

"Eighteen people vying for three spots," said Allen.

"Not bad. You two will have this mess behind you before you know it."

"Yes. Hopefully." Allen pulled a folder off his desk and scanned the contents. "It's an interesting mix of people. Not sure how these folks will handle themselves as we get closer to the end. Brewster, Carson, Early, Goodwell, Lockhart, Peasley—"

"Wait—did you say Goodwell? As in Starlight?"

Allen peered at the sheet. "It says Linda here, but she goes by Starlight, doesn't she?"

"Yes." Greg moved to look over Allen's shoulder. "She's on the list? Since when?"

"Since the beginning, as far as I know."

"You're kidding!"

"Is that a problem?" asked Ambrose.

Greg didn't answer. He stood there and simmered, feeling like a kitchen knife had just been plunged into his back.

CHAPTER 15

"Well, this is a surprise! To what do I owe the honor of this unannounced visit?" Starlight greeted Greg warmly at her front door.

"Can we talk?" Greg didn't feel like returning the warmth.

"Uh, OK. Sure." She waved him in.

Starlight sat in her easy chair while Greg stood.

"Why didn't you tell me that you're on the waiting list?"

"Oh. That. Greg, please sit down. You look so tense you're making *me* tense." Greg plopped into the couch and crossed his arms.

"I can't believe you've been on the list the whole time and never once mentioned it to me."

"I can't believe you didn't know about it already. You've been in on this list thing since day one. I just assumed you knew."

"I—" He was confounded by her nonchalance. "I—guess I never looked at it closely. It was pretty long at first. That doesn't explain why you've led me on for months."

"Led you on?"

"Yes."

She rested her chin on her hand with a smug grin. "How exactly have I led you on?"

"Every time the subject has come up, you've talked as if you weren't part of them." His voice was rising, as was the pulsing in his chest.

"Who?"

"The people on the list. The people we've been mocking for months. You always talk about 'them,' but this whole time your name was on the list right next to theirs."

"So?"

"It doesn't make any sense."

"Why not?"

"Because you're not one of them!" He didn't mean to yell, and he regretted it the instant he saw her wince. She answered softly.

"No. I'm not. I guess you're right about that. Thanks for the reminder."

His frustration was wilting. "That's not what I meant. That came out wrong."

She shrugged it off. "We both know it's true, Greg."

"What I'm trying to say is that you're not like them . . . in a good way. You—you're better than that. You're not shallow and pretentious. Haven't we joked about the people in this town for the last two years?"

She didn't answer. He started to feel ashamed at how condescending he sounded.

"I'm sorry I upset you, Greg. I didn't mean to do that."

"I'm not upset. I'm confused. I mean, is this really something you want? A place in Cotterman? You've said the whole thing is silly and stupid."

"Just 'cause something is silly doesn't mean it's not worth doing."

"Seriously?"

She mulled over her next words carefully, then spoke with a solemnity Greg had never heard from her before.

"I know it makes you uncomfortable when people are overly transparent with you, so I'll give you the short version." Though he was fairly sure she hadn't meant this as an insult, his throat tightened in reaction. "For most of my life, I've lived minute to minute. I've never been a planner or a forward thinker. Didn't have the luxury of time.

"Even when I met Everett, got married, and moved here. I hadn't really thought the whole thing through, to be honest. Don't get me wrong! I loved him. I still do. I miss him a lot, and now that he's gone it feels like all I have is time. I'm pretty much by myself here at the house. Solitude breeds a deeper level of contemplation, I suppose."

"But Everett's been gone for a while. Why the sudden change of heart?" Greg worked to keep his words calm and caring.

"It's not a change of heart as much as it's an acceptance of reality. I'm gonna be pushing sixty before too long. I've got no plans to move. Don't even know where I would go. My prospects for a change in status are slim to none. That's not a ploy for pity, it's just the truth. I guess you could say that, for the first time in my life, I'm trying to make a plan. An estate plan!" She winked.

He'd come to her house with a fervent intention to talk her into dropping off the waiting list. Now, it would be incredibly tacky to pursue this. He ran his fingers through his hair and forced a smile.

"There's just one problem with your plan."

"What's that?"

"You may be pushing sixty, but that still puts you a good ten years behind everyone else on that list. Statistically speaking, you don't stand a chance of getting one of those last three spots."

"Well, there you go. No harm, no foul, right?"

"I'm pretty sure somebody around here won't see it that generously. Probably several somebodies. You're gonna ruffle some feathers if word gets out that you're on the list."

"You think people don't already know?"

"I assume most don't know."

"Well, look at it this way. If I don't get one of the spots, no one will be the wiser. If by some weird miracle I do get one —" She looked out the front window toward the center of town. "Nothing like a big surprise at a funeral to spice things up, right?"

He stood. "I gotta get going."

She rose, too. "I'm sorry I threw a monkey wrench into things. If I'd known it would upset you, I'd have told you long ago."

"Would I have been able to talk you out of it?"

"Probably not."

"You didn't do anything wrong. It's just me. I really like to know where I stand."

She put her hand on his shoulder, looking him squarely in the eyes.

"When it comes to me, if you wanna know where you stand all you gotta do is ask. I'll tell you."

Phil Lockhart passed away in early May, claiming the next plot. The number of those still hoping for Cotterman spots dropped to eleven. When Frank Erickson suffered a massive stroke a month later, four people deleted their names from the list because it looked like the cemetery was down to its final resting place.

But Frank didn't die. Though the stroke had debilitated him irreparably, he clung to the last threads of life in an ICU out in Scranton.

"How long do you think he'll hang on in this coma?" Gladys asked during lunch at the office.

"How would I know?" Greg snapped back.

"You're the M.D. You must have some opinion about it."

"I haven't seen Frank or his chart so I'm in no position to offer any predictions. These things can go on for months. Sometimes years."

"I wonder if the family is thinking about pulling the

plug." Gladys clucked her tongue in disapproval. "This is why DNRs are such a good idea. My husband and I both have one."

"Isn't it a bit early to be thinking of that?"

"Never too early, Doc. You should know that."

"Yeah."

As Frank persisted in staying alive, people began to calculate the wait-list odds in earnest. Though Ambrose, Allen, and Greg kept the remaining names a strict secret, town gossip deduced them anyway.

Frank passed away, still in the coma, after several weeks. By then, all Emmitsville knew the identities of the final three contenders.

Archie Early, Opal Ridgley, and Starlight Goodwell.

CHAPTER 16

"*T*hey're all as different as can be," Betty commented one morning as Greg waited near Gladys's desk for a fax to come through.

"Yes, they are," said Gladys. "Archie's friendly and flirty and one of the nicest people you'll meet. Opal . . . she's . . ."

"She's a bitch."

"Betty!"

"Sorry." Betty's apology belied the mischief in her eyes. "I meant to say *witch*."

"That's not much better."

"Oh, come on! You know I'm right. In all the years she's been coming in here has she ever shown the slightest hint of kindness to you?"

Gladys thought it over. "Not really, but Dr. Greg spends more time with her than I do. What do you say, Doctor?"

Greg had been staring at the fax machine hoping that his fax would come through before either woman looped him into their discussion, but the machine remained silent and uncooperative.

"Opal? She's . . ."

"See?" Betty seized on Greg's hesitation. "She's the town witch! He's just too polite to say it!"

"I was going to say that she prefers to keep to herself." He gave up on the fax and walked toward his office, hearing their comments right up until he closed the door.

"All I'm saying is that it's really no wonder her husband left her."

"Goodness! It's been ages since he left. Just a couple of months after I moved here."

Greg didn't linger to hear what they had to say about Starlight.

Just as he'd feared, disapproval over Starlight's presence on the list abounded in all corners, though few were willing to come right out and say what they were thinking—she didn't deserve a one-in-three chance to complete the cycle of burials in Cotterman.

"I'm just happy that no one has talked to you about it directly," Greg confessed to her. "People can be downright nasty when they want to."

Starlight jutted out her chin in defiance. "Don't you worry. I can handle myself. They can say and think whatever they want."

Despite significant pressure on her to give up, Starlight held her ground. Once it was clear that she intended to stick it out until the end, Emmitsville was left in the same position as before—waiting for someone to die or for another occurrence to shake up the status quo.

That happened in early August, when Greg strolled into the office one morning to find Gladys in the hallway.

"Doctor! I'm glad you're here!" She sounded a little breathless. "I think you better sit down."

"Why?"

"I heard some news this morning, and . . . you're not going to like it."

Her tone and the tightness in her face reminded him of when she'd told him about his father. He thought of Sandy— they hadn't talked in several months.

"What's wrong?"

"Opal Ridgley is—"

Greg's cell phone chirped in his pocket. After consulting the screen, he slipped past Gladys and answered just as he closed the office door behind him.

"Hello?"

"I just got a phone call from a lawyer representing Opal Ridgley. She's filed a lawsuit against us!"

It was Ambrose. He didn't have much specific information to offer. Opal was attempting to circumvent the natural order and take ownership of the final burial plot through a judge. Greg adopted the air of calmness and reasonableness he'd used so many times with the Wannamakers over the previous months.

"Sounds to me like she's really reaching. I can't imagine a judge taking this seriously."

"Are you kidding? Judges take on ridiculous lawsuits all the time. You read about them practically every day."

"Well, even so . . . she won't win. How could she? How could she possibly convince the judge to accept her claim over Archie's and Starlight's? How would that be fair?"

"I don't know, but I've got an awful feeling in the pit of my stomach. To take this to court? Air the whole thing out in public even more? It's sickening, Greg. It'll be simply awful."

Greg couldn't summon any more platitudes. He knew that Ambrose's fears were well-founded. Opal seemed to be the type who would approach the lawsuit in a chilling, calculated style that would drag the funeral home and the brothers through a humiliating spectacle. That was probably the whole point.

After the call, Greg tapped the intercom button on his office phone. "I know you're waiting."

Gladys entered and sat on the other side of the desk.

"So?" She looked more curious and far less concerned

than when Greg first walked into the office that morning. "Is it true what I heard? Was that Ambrose?"

"Yes and yes."

"Wow. She's really doing it. It's a bold move."

"It's a ridiculous move. Arrogant and completely out of line."

"I knew you'd be upset."

"More like irritated and shocked. It never occurred to me that she'd go off like this."

"It might work."

Greg shook his head emphatically. "Not if it never gets off the ground."

"What are you talking about?"

"As soon as I'm done with patients today I'm going out and putting a stop to all this. Enough is enough."

"How do you plan to do that?"

"With the powers of persuasion and common sense."

She stifled a laugh when she realized he meant it.

That afternoon, Greg turned the corner onto Starlight's street and saw a white sports car in her driveway. He drove by slowly and parked in the road. As he walked past the car, admiring it, he heard the front door squeak shut.

Archie Early sauntered down the driveway. "Good afternoon, Doc!"

Greg shook the tall, spindly gentleman's hand.

"Hi, Archie. What are you doing here?"

"Oh, I just swung by for a visit. How about you?"

"Pretty much the same. Just swinging by."

Archie tilted his head toward the front door. "From what she tells me, you do that pretty regularly."

"Starlight?"

"Yessir. She says you stop by most every week. Says it's always a real nice time for you both."

Greg reddened, and he swallowed. "Yes, it's—we play cards usually."

"I guess that makes two of us, then. For the visiting, I mean. We usually do more talking than playing."

"Listen, Archie, I'm glad to run into you. I was going to come see you later or give you a call."

"Yup. Starlight said you'd be coming around."

Greg sputtered. "I—didn't tell her I was coming."

"I know." Archie smiled. "She was just guessing. She's a pretty good guesser."

"I want to talk to you about—"

"—about the lawsuit. She guessed that part too."

Greg tried to regain his composure. "Don't you think this cemetery business has gone on long enough?"

"What makes you say that?"

"Come on, Archie." Greg's patience for pleasantries was gone. "We've officially reached the point of ridiculous. The whole thing is like some overplayed melodrama. A lawsuit? Really?"

Archie shrugged. "It's not *my* lawsuit."

"I know, but it's still a lawsuit. It will take up time. It'll tie up a courtroom. It will be a nightmare for Ambrose and Allen. Is it really worth all of that?"

"You say this as if it's my doing, Doctor, but like I said— it's not my case. Seems to me you should be talking to Opal instead."

"You could pull out of the running. Take your name off the list. Starlight, too. If no one else is vying for the last spot, there's no need for a lawsuit, right?"

"So what you're saying is we pull out and basically give the spot to Opal outright. Is that how you see it?"

"Makes sense to me."

Archie slid his hands into the pockets of his jeans. "I don't think I'll do that, but thanks for the idea, Doc. I mean it. You're a good guy. You care about folks. Especially those Wannamaker brothers. I know you're just trying to get them out of this pickle, and I admire your effort."

"It's not about being kind or helping the Wannamakers, Archie. It's about what's right."

"Come again? That's a bit lofty, wouldn't you say? Who says Opal's right and I'm wrong?"

"No, that's not what I mean."

"Well, then who says *you're* right and the rest of us are wrong?" Archie's manner had begun to feel strained.

"That didn't come out the way I wanted it to. It's—it's more about what's best. What really matters in the long run. Does that make sense?"

"So, tell me. What really matters in the long run, Doctor?" Archie stared him in the eyes with uncharacteristic directness.

"Look. I wasn't trying to upset you. I probably stepped out of line, and I'm sorry. You should do what you feel is best."

Archie's smile returned, and he reached out to shake Greg's hand. "That's something you can count on, Doc. Have yourself a nice day."

Starlight opened her door just as Archie was backing his car out of the driveway.

"Hi, Greg! Right on time!" She held out her hands with a smile. "So? Go ahead and let me have it."

"Have what?"

"A slap on the wrist. That's why you came over, isn't it? I butted in, upset everyone, and probably pushed Opal over the edge. Now, she's going to court and you're worried the whole thing is going to turn into some circus. You're here to ream me out and convince me to change my mind, right?"

"You got most of it right."

They sat on the couch, and Starlight turned to him. "What did I miss?"

"The whole thing already is a circus. The lawsuit only means it'll get worse."

"It might get better. You never know."

"How could it possibly get better?"

"OK. At the very least, it might get more interesting. You gotta admit. The lawsuit angle is intriguing at least."

"I don't have to admit anything."

She shoved his arm playfully. "Wow, this really did get you grouchy, didn't it?"

Her touch felt oddly reassuring, and her flirty tone softened the edge of his anger. He'd driven there with an agenda, but he'd lost his passion for the fight.

"Is there anything I can say to get you to give up?"

"I'm sure there probably is somewhere in the universe, but nothing comes to mind. I've thrown my hat in the ring, and I'm going to keep it there. Might as well."

"Well, maybe the judge will bring some sense into all of this and dismiss the case before it gets off the ground."

"You can hope."

"Trust me, I do."

CHAPTER 17

*T*he Court of Common Pleas dashed Greg's hopes and accepted Opal's lawsuit. But a week later, Opal changed course. The logjammed bureaucracy of the county court system was slowing the case to an extent she found unacceptable. The clerk informed both parties that it would likely take at least six months to get an initial hearing before the judge, so Opal tried a new tactic—mediation.

The Wannamakers agreed to sit down with her and a professional mediator to see if an agreement could be reached outside of court. It couldn't. Opal was unwilling to concede anything, and the Wannamakers couldn't bring themselves to ignore the other two names on the list and give her the only thing she really wanted.

The case went quiet for a few weeks. Ambrose checked with the courthouse several times to see if Opal had withdrawn her complaint, but the lawsuit was still on the docket.

Starlight theorized to Greg, "She's hoping Archie and me will just get tired of waiting and give up."

"Will you?"

"Not planning on it. Why would we? Even if she does make it into a courtroom, I don't believe the judge will give it to her. It's arrogant to think that her claim is somehow more valid than ours. It's no skin off our nose to keep waiting."

Greg wasn't so certain about Opal losing the case. She'd always struck him as being subtle but stubborn. If she was able to get in front of a judge, she would likely use any dirty tricks she could to go full bore at Ambrose and Allen.

But then, at the end of August, she reached out through her lawyer to request a meeting with Starlight and Archie. Starlight asked Greg to go with her.

"I'm not a lawyer. I'm a physician."

She smirked at him. "Yes, Greg, I'm well aware of the fact."

"Why take me with you?"

"I don't want a lawyer with me. Don't think I'll need one. I'd rather have you. I need a date for the big show!"

"Is that what this meeting is?"

"I don't know what it is, but I'm curious to find out. Aren't you?"

He rolled into her driveway at nine o'clock on the morning of the meeting. When she scurried out to the car, he noticed she was wearing bright colors and had curled her hair.

"You're ready, huh?"

"Yessir! Let's do this."

It was less than an hour's drive to Scranton. Inside a tan office building on the east side of the city, Greg and Starlight made their way to a conference room on the first floor. Archie and his lawyer were already seated at the huge, elliptical wooden table. Nondescript artwork hung in cheap frames on the walls, and a solitary water cooler stood in a corner.

Archie's smile lit up. "Starlight! Good morning!" He greeted her with an encompassing embrace. Greg noticed that his right hand lingered on the small of her back as he guided her into the chair next to his.

"This is Reggie Hamilton. My attorney." Starlight shook

hands with the finely suited man on the other side of Archie. "Doc? You doing some moonlighting as a lawyer these days?"

Greg sat down next to Starlight. "Nope. Just a spectator. Starlight asked me to come."

"Well, now, things keep gettin' more interesting all the time, don't they?"

A short woman with wide shoulders and long, straight hair walked in. She wore a dark suit and carried a stack of folders under one arm.

"Good morning, everyone." She circled around to a seat directly opposite them. "Thank you all for coming today."

Archie verbalized what everyone else was thinking. "Where's Opal?"

The woman set the folders down on the table. "Miss Ridgley will not be attending this meeting. My name is Monica Sachs. I'm her attorney. I'll be making the offer on her behalf."

"Offer?" asked Starlight.

Monica smiled. "Yes. Of course. Let's get right to it so as to waste no one's time. Miss Ridgely has asked me to inform you—though we feel she has a valid case with strong evidence for the supremacy of her claim to the burial plot in Cotterman Cemetery—she understands that a lengthy court battle with the Wannamakers is in no one's best interest. She believes a speedy resolution to this rather unique situation is beneficial for all involved."

She pulled two folders off the top of the stack and slid one in front of Starlight and the other to Archie.

"The offer is as follows: Miss Ridgley is prepared to give each of you a substantial amount of money in exchange for you officially withdrawing your name from the list for the final plot in the cemetery."

"How substantial?" asked Starlight.

"If both of you agree to the terms of her offer, Miss Ridgley has authorized me to issue each of you a check today in the amount of 75,000 dollars." Monica paused, as if waiting for a dramatic response from the other side of the table, but Archie's lawyer interposed. "What are the terms?"

Monica didn't acknowledge the question. She kept her gaze on Starlight and Archie. "To receive the money, you must agree to the following five things. One, you must contact the funeral home today and instruct them to remove your name from the list. Two, you must sign a written agreement stating that you relinquish all claims to the final burial plot. Three, you must sign a nondisclosure agreement—"

Archie jumped in. "Nondisclosure about what?"

"About anything related to the offer we are currently discussing. Four, you must *both* agree to her offer or there is no deal. And five, you must decide whether or not you will accept her terms today . . . before you leave. The offer is invalid after that."

"What's the big rush?" Starlight chuckled. "Is she afraid one of us is gonna drop dead by dinnertime?"

Monica was steadfastly deadpan. "The likelihood might be small, but the reality is that the status quo leaves my client in a position of losing the plot if something catastrophic happens to either of you. That's a risk she is unwilling to assume, and—as I already mentioned—she feels that a quick resolution to this dilemma is in everyone's best interest."

"So if we don't take her offer . . ." Starlight prompted.

"She has not ruled out the possibility of continuing with or expanding upon the legal action she's already set in motion."

Starlight and Archie looked at each other closely.

Monica continued, "Despite the urgent nature of the offer, I know you'll need some time to consider it. All of the details are spelled out in the paper work. I'll step down the hall so you can discuss."

When she was gone, Starlight leaned back and let out a

loud sigh. "Wow! Did you catch that? Take the money today or what? She's gonna sue us?" She directed the question to Archie, but Reggie answered.

"There's nothing she can sue you over. Not that I know of."

"What do you think, Reg?" Archie asked as Reggie scanned the documentation.

"So far it looks straightforward. Give up your place on the list. Promise to keep quiet. Get the money. It seems as simple as that."

Archie swiveled his chair toward Starlight. "What about you?"

"I'm wondering why she didn't try this earlier. Like months ago? It's not a bad approach." She shrugged. "Maybe she couldn't afford to buy out so many people."

"Oh, she can afford it. I can assure you of that. When she and Robert divorced, she made sure she got her piece of the pie and a little extra, from what I heard. She used that same lawyer lady back then. The two of them—they're a tenacious team." Archie called out to Greg, who had left his chair and was staring at one of the paintings on the wall. "What d'ya say, Doc?"

Greg didn't turn around. "The offer is . . . intriguing. She's not leaving anything to chance. Trying to wrap the whole thing up in one swoop."

"Greg and Reggie, would you mind giving me and Archie the room? I think we need to talk this over."

In the hallway, Reggie leaned against the wall and continued reading from Archie's folder.

"Isn't this the craziest thing?" Greg ventured.

"What is?" Reggie didn't look up.

"This offer. The cemetery."

Reggie spoke briskly. "It's odd, but I've seen worse. In my experience, people want what they want. When they want it badly enough they'll do just about anything you can imagine to get it."

"I suppose that's true."

Greg excused himself to find a restroom. Two doors down from the conference room, he stopped short. Through the doorway, he saw Opal sitting on a small tan couch.

"Opal! Hi! Your lawyer said you weren't—"

"I'm waiting. To hear what they decide." She spoke softly, looking apprehensive.

"Oh. Well—"

"I'm fully aware of how you feel about all this, Doctor. I don't need you to tell me how shallow and pretentious I am."

He didn't see any reason for her vitriol. It irritated him, but he tried to play it off lightly.

"Actually, I was going to say that your approach—your offer—is an intriguing way to handle this."

"To be quite candid, I find you confusing."

"You find *me* confusing?"

"Your actions. You've made it clear to me how preposterous you find the Cotterman situation to be, yet it seems you've been involved in it from the beginning."

He inched further into the room. "Kinda got roped into it."

"I find that hard to believe."

"Why is that?"

"You're not the kind of person who gets 'roped into' things, Doctor." She shook her head emphatically. "If you're involved, it's because you want to be."

"I feel like you're jumping to all sorts of conclusions about me, Opal, and I don't understand why."

"I guess we have that in common, at least. You and everyone else pointing fingers at me. Criticizing. Thinking you know me. My motives. *Why does she have to make it such a big deal? Why won't she just let it play out on its own?*"

Greg leaned back against the doorframe. "Why don't you?"

"Pardon me?"

"I'm not trying to be a jerk, but I really wonder. Why go through all of this? You're offering to give up 150,000 dollars on the spot just to get . . . what? A hole in the ground?"

"I wouldn't expect someone like you to understand."

"I've been your physician for over a decade. I think of us as friends. I'm not some stranger, Opal. You know me. Maybe you could give me the benefit of the doubt."

"I've talked with you many times. I've seen you in Emmitsville all these years. That's why I don't expect you to understand, Doctor. You live here, but you're untethered. You've never connected to this place. It's like you float above the town and only swoop down from time to time to make sure we're all still breathing."

Her potshots were stretching his ability to keep from lashing back at her. "Maybe that's something else we have in common. Living at arm's length?"

"It hasn't always been that way. I've been in Emmitsville since I was eleven. I raised a family there. I've lived most of my life in that valley. My parents and my siblings are buried in Cotterman. For decades I've had to endure the indignity of being excluded from . . ."

She trailed off, leaving Greg to wonder about what she'd left unsaid.

"Now, to see an opportunity for some redemption just within reach—well, like I said. I don't really expect you to understand."

"I understand that Emmitsville and Cotterman mean a lot to you. I get that. But here's what I can't wrap my mind around. Is it really worth all the trouble? Seriously, Opal. If you get the last spot—one way or the other—will it be worth all the stress and conflict it took to get there? When you're dead and gone?"

"I don't know, Doctor. I guess I'll have to wait and see." She looked him in the eyes and spoke evenly. "But tell me this. When *you* are dead and gone, will it be worth all of your effort to convince yourself that it's not?"

"I guess I'll have to wait and see as well."

"Then it seems we have several things in common. If you'll excuse me now, I think I'd prefer to be left alone."

When Greg returned to the conference room, Starlight was standing at the door.

"There you are!" She met him in the hallway. "Reggie and Archie are in there looking things over again."

"What are you going to do?"

"Archie seems to be holding his ground. He doesn't need the money, and—despite what my humble surroundings might indicate—I don't either. He thinks we should send her on her way with her folders and her checks."

"What do you think?"

"I'm torn."

"Really?"

"Why do you sound so surprised?"

"I thought you were in this thing for the duration. Gonna watch it all play out."

"I still want to, but I've been thinking since we got here. Maybe you're right."

He smirked. "Miracles do happen!"

She slugged him playfully on the arm. "I'm serious! Maybe it's time to put the whole thing to rest. Let Opal have the last plot and move on."

"That will only work if both you and Archie agree to it, remember?"

"What do you think we should do?"

"It doesn't matter what I think. It's not my decision."

"But what's your opinion? I'm sure you've got one."

Greg turned slightly and looked toward the doorway of

the room where Opal was waiting. The sting of her tone was still roiling him.

"What's wrong?" Starlight asked.

"Nothing." Greg turned back to look at her. "I think you should do whatever you want."

"You do?"

"I get the feeling you've lived most of your life that way." It was his turn to playfully poke her in the shoulder. "Why stop now?"

"I figured you'd tell me to end the whole thing right away. Take the money and run!" She started back toward the conference room. "You are a complicated fellow, Dr. Patterson. I haven't quite figured you out yet. I'm gonna go check back with Archie."

Greg stayed in the hallway while Starlight and Archie deliberated.

Opal's lawyer returned a while later, and both Archie and Starlight gave flat refusals to the offer. Monica looked surprised and disappointed.

"I see. I'll let Miss Ridgley know about your decision. Rest assured that we will contact you if there are any further developments on our end."

Once she was out of the room Archie, Starlight, and Reggie discussed possible meanings of the phrase *further developments* while Greg moved casually toward the door. He leaned out just enough to see down the hallway. At the far end of the corridor, he glimpsed Opal and her lawyer walking slowly around the corner and out of sight.

CHAPTER 18

"*S*he baffles me," Greg announced as his car rolled to a stop in front of Starlight's house.

"Opal? Yeah, but most people baffle you."

"What makes you say that?"

"It's true, isn't it?"

"To some extent, I guess."

"Well, there you go. Oh, don't worry about it, Doctor! They say it's a sign of high intelligence."

"What is?"

"Social ineptitude."

"You think I'm socially inept?"

She laughed. "I'll put it this way—I wouldn't expect either of us to win any popularity awards."

"Fine with me. Saves me from having to attend an awards dinner."

"It's too bad. We could've gone together. I would've gotten all dolled up for it!" She pulled her purse up from the floor beside her feet. "You got a busy day ahead?"

"Not really. I asked Gladys not to schedule anything. I wasn't sure how long we'd be gone."

"You wanna come in for some tea or a snack or something?"

They sat in her small kitchen, Starlight with an oversized mug of tea and Greg with a tall glass of ice water. She had set out a tin of shortbread cookies, and they both kept reaching in to grab another as they talked for nearly an hour.

"Will you excuse me for a moment? I need to see a man about a horse." Starlight stood up. "I've never understood that saying."

"Me neither."

She went down the hall. Greg stared at her mug of tea. He noticed a trace of her lipstick on the rim.

"Whatcha thinking?"

He startled. "Oh! Just thinking about being socially inept."

She was standing next to his chair. "I was just kidding about that, Greg. Please don't—"

"No, it's true. I know it is. Been that way most of my life. Not sure why."

She looked down at him with compassion.

"I was just sitting here thinking." Greg gestured toward the kitchen and the living room across the hall with an arcing sweep of his hand. "Other than my apartment and my office, this is one of the few places where I feel completely comfortable. At ease."

"You really feel that way?"

"Yeah." He joked, "You should feel honored."

She sat down again and spoke sincerely. "I'm happy you enjoy being in my home. I love having you here. Your visits mean a lot to me. They encourage me probably more than you realize."

"I'm glad." He shifted in his chair and took a gulp of water. "You know, it's funny. When Summer met you all those months ago, she mentioned . . ."

Starlight dug another cookie out of the tin. "She mentioned what?"

"She thinks that—" He drummed his fingers on the table

and finally mumbled, "I guess she's not the only one to think it."

"Greg, you're not making any sense."

Greg despised outbursts, and rarely was he subject to fits of impulse. He liked to think before he spoke—afraid of saying the wrong thing. For most of his life, his behavior had been practiced, even calculating.

But in that moment he yielded to a rush of spontaneity and reached across the table for her hand.

"I've been thinking about something, for months, actually, and I wanted to ask—"

"What is happening right now?" Her eyes were wide.

Greg felt his stomach knot up. "I . . . um . . ."

She slipped her hand from his. "Greg . . . oh, crap!"

They looked away from each other.

Starlight broke the silence. "One of us should say something, I guess."

Greg didn't look up from the tabletop. "I think . . . it would be easier if I just left. I've put you in an awkward position and—"

"No! Don't leave, please. I'll do the talking."

Greg felt her looking at him, and he slowly raised his eyes to meet her gaze—a gentle mixture of sadness and reluctance.

"Greg . . . you're my friend. Probably the best one I have right now, but . . . that's all. To me, that's all it is. I can't . . . it can't be more than that."

Greg nodded. "OK. Fair enough."

"Please don't shut down on me, OK? It's just that—I don't open myself up to many people. When I do, I guess I have the tendency to open way up. You know what I mean? If I let my hair down, I tend to let it all the way down. I think that can make me come across in a way I don't intend."

"Yeah. I get it. Makes sense."

"Does it really?"

He tried to mask his overwhelming disappointment. "I

got the wrong impression. I let my brain run away from me, and I made things uncomfortable for both of us. I'm sorry. Hopefully, we can just move on and pretend I never said anything."

She continued to look squarely at him. "I can do that. Can you?"

"Why couldn't I?"

"You don't seem like you're good at pretending something never happened."

He slapped the table with his palm. "Why does everyone think they're some sort of expert in the nuances of my psyche?" He immediately regretted his outburst. "I'm sorry. I'm . . . I'm sorry. I think I need to leave."

"You can stay. I'd like you to stay."

"Can I ask you something?"

"That depends on what it is." She smiled and winked— her attempt to walk back the tension between them.

He responded in kind. "You're safe, I promise. Purely intellectual motives."

"Go for it."

"You said that we're friends—and I agree—but you also said you'd never see me as more than that."

"No, I said it could never be more than that."

"Same thing."

"There's a huge difference!"

"Whatever. I don't want to squabble over semantics. My question is—why say it so . . . conclusively?"

"You want to know if it's you or if it's me." She sipped from her mug and conjured up an answer. "It's both."

"Come again?"

"It's both of us."

"That's . . . that's convenient."

"And it's true. I'm not just being nice. The reason we have to stay what we are is because it's you and me we're talking about." She leaned forward. "Greg, you're a great guy. I know that sounds trite, but you are. You're funny, smart, attractive. I'd be lying if I said certain thoughts haven't crossed my mind more than once over the years."

"But . . . ?"

"But you're not truly available."

"You mean like in an emotional sense?"

"No. I mean in a real sense. You're not available. You're married."

"Technically." He remembered his conversation with Summer months earlier about the same thing. His loyalty to the idea of his marriage was significantly less now as he sat across from Starlight.

"So . . . that's a deal breaker for me."

He thought it over. "What if Alicia and I never get back together? It's been fifteen years. If it hasn't happened by now—"

"Do you want to get back together?"

"I'm not sure. I miss her in a lot of ways, but it just got to be too much."

"The gap got too wide." Greg nodded in agreement. "Who says you can't cover that distance?"

"It's not entirely up to me. There are some details about our separation I haven't mentioned yet."

"You haven't mentioned any details—not specifically."

"The short version is that Alicia went through a real rough patch back then. Some of it was physical, some emotional. Mental-health kind of stuff. I didn't step up the way I needed to. The way I should have. I guess she started to feel like she couldn't depend on me, like I broke her trust. Even if I reached out, I'm not sure she'd take me back."

"You won't know unless you try."

"Yes, but neither of us seems headed in that direction. I think we've gotten too comfortable apart from each other. Set in our ways."

"That might be true or it might not. But I don't want to be

the thing that keeps it from happening if it's supposed to happen. Know what I mean?"

"What about you? You said it's both of us. What's your deal?"

She raised an eyebrow. "Well! Aren't we bold in our questions today?" Despite her jesting, Greg could see she hesitated to answer. "There's a lot to it. A lot to . . . me."

"Tell me something I don't know already," he said with a smile.

"All right. How about this?" Her eyes darkened a bit. "I don't want to keep you and Alicia from getting back together because . . . I've played that role before, and I don't ever want to do it again. I can't. It's just too awful."

"The role of . . . ?"

"The other woman."

"Oh."

"How much do you know about Everett and me?"

"Only what you've told me."

"And?"

He knew exactly what she was fishing for, but he didn't want to say it. "And . . . what I've heard from others."

"Ah, yes! There it is. What have you heard?"

He shrugged. "Lots of things."

"The truth is somewhere in the middle, I suppose. The truth is that Everett came into my life at a time when I was on the edge. In a way, he rescued me. I'm thankful for him every day that I wake up. But that doesn't make it any easier knowing that I destroyed his marriage. We didn't have an affair—at least—not in the traditional sense. I want to be sure you know that."

"OK."

"Before Emmitsville, I lived on the north side of Chicago. I was on the edge—barely scraping by. It was very difficult for me to find a job because of—reasons. I ended up as a waitress at a seedy place downtown.

"This was the kind of place where most of the customers were men, looking for more than just a meal. The whole place had that testosterone, libido feel to it, you know?" She didn't look him in the eye. "After a while as a waitress there, you figure out that—there's opportunity for more if you're willing to take it. I guess you could call it a side hustle."

"Seriously?"

"I'm not proud of it. It's just the kind of thing that happens . . . if you let it. And I did. Quite a few times. It was dangerous and stupid."

Greg felt uncomfortable. He didn't know what to say.

"Here's the thing. I did it because it felt like the only way I could get some traction in my life. Believe it or not, it was one of the few times when I felt powerful. In control. These guys were repressed husbands traveling on business or lonely singles in their thirties stopping by after a tough day at the office. All of them sending out vibes. All of them looking to live out some macho story of conquest or something stupid like that. The truth is they were just a bunch of wimps who felt so guilty afterward that they'd usually give me cash right there in the room or run to an ATM."

Greg gave a measured response. "Jeez. That's—I'm sorry for you."

"It's been a long time. It happened. I can't change any of it now, so I don't waste much time on it. And it's how I met Everett, so . . . there's a silver lining, so to speak."

"Is that where the nontraditional affair comes in?"

"Yes. About a year and a half after I started at the restaurant I met Everett. He said he'd seen me several times before, but I don't remember. One Tuesday night, I waited on his table. He wrote the name of his hotel and room number on the credit-card slip before he left."

"That seems . . . on the nose."

Starlight laughed sardonically. "It's more common than you think. That and the old 'Here's my business card' bit."

"I guess I just never thought of being so forward."

"You're such a good boy, Greg," she prodded lightly.

"That's not what I meant."

"Anyway, I'm really ashamed about this but—Everett seemed like the kind of opportunity that could pay off. He was older than most of the other customers, and he carried himself in a way that made me think, *This guy's loaded*. I was right. He certainly didn't fit in with everyone else. It wasn't his kind of place at all."

"Then why was he there?"

"Beats me. I never asked him. Everett did unexpected things sometimes for no apparent reason—even after we were married he was like that. After my shift I went to his hotel, and things got even weirder."

"Oh, you can skip that part."

"No, you don't get it. Nothing happened. We didn't have sex. I don't think he had that in mind at all. I didn't even go to his room. We spent a couple of hours talking in the hotel bar. He bought me dinner. We had a few drinks. I kept expecting him to invite me up, but he never did. He just told me stories from his life and asked lots of questions about mine. Then he slipped me some cash and called me a taxi. That was it. Until the next time."

"This happened more than once?"

"We met like that at least a dozen times over the next two years. He'd fly into town every three months for business. He'd stop by and invite me to his hotel. I was really skeptical the first few times. Kept waiting for the other shoe to drop. I guess I was expecting him to be a creep like all the other men. It took me seven or eight visits to trust that his intentions were harmless and simple. He just wanted someone to talk to. And he'd give me a boost of cash. It was a strange arrangement, but I got to the point where his visits were the highlight of my week—my month! And not just because of the money."

Greg cut in. "I didn't think that was the case."

"Yeah, you did. Don't worry! Most anybody would. Heck! It *was* about the money—for the first year. Then I realized it was about more. I could get money from the losers I waited on every night. Everett was different. I genuinely enjoyed him as a person. He cared about me, and I cared about him." She sounded almost poetic. "It was innocent. Pure. One of the few things in my life that wasn't completely screwed up."

"So . . . ?"

"How did I destroy his marriage? I didn't intend to. I had asked him about his wife—about how she'd react if she knew about us. He fluffed it off each time. Said she barely noticed him as it was. I didn't let myself think any more about it until she found out."

"How'd that happen?"

"Everett. He straight out told her the whole story one day. I think he was feeling guilty. Not about me, but about keeping it from her. He tried to explain that it was nothing but companionship."

"Did that work?"

"What do you think? She was furious. The marriage tore apart instantly. He tried to make it quick and painless, but she let him have it with everything she could. And she started a bunch of rumors about me. You know what's kind of funny about that? I never met Alice. Not once. Never even saw her from a distance. The closest I ever got was pictures I saw on the wall when I moved in with Everett." Remorse washed over her face. "That was enough, though. It was absolute torture knowing I'd torn that family apart. Their son refused to meet me. Everett lost a good chunk of his fortune in the divorce. I mean, we still had enough to live more comfortably than I'd ever imagined, but I damaged his life forever. All of their lives."

"Everett bears at least some of the responsibility, wouldn't you say?"

Starlight gave the barest nod of her head, and tipped up the mug to swallow the last of her tea.

"So, Dr. Patterson, that—along with a few other reasons— is why I think it's best if we limit ourselves to a platonic relationship. Peppy but platonic."

The flow of the conversation and her carefree tone had eased his mood, though conflicting emotions still pulsed in his temples and chest.

"Peppy platonic, huh?"

"You OK with that?" She was watching him closely, with a touch of uncertainty in her eyes.

"Yeah. I'm OK with that. I feel bad for even bringing it up."

"Don't be. Our afternoon wouldn't have been nearly as interesting."

He stood. "I should probably get going for real this time. I do have one more question."

"I'll allow it, but after this you've reached your limit."

They were at her front door, and he stood with one hand on the doorknob. "Why did you tell me all of that? About your past. You didn't have to. Especially with such hard memories."

"You asked."

"Fair enough."

"Why did you stay? You were ready to bolt. You didn't have to stick around."

His thoughts were too jumbled to answer right away.

"I stayed because I wanted to."

"I'm glad."

He hugged her, lightly circling her shoulders in his arms and feeling wisps of her hair brush against his neck.

"Enjoy your afternoon, Starlight."

"You too, Doc. I'll see you soon."

CHAPTER 19

*A*nother stifling, stagnant Emmitsville summer came to a close without incident as far as Cotterman was concerned. While the townsfolk held on to their morbid curiosity about who would occupy the last scrap of cemetery, the controversy was now nearly a year old and had lost its sensational luster.

Greg never told Starlight about his conversation with Opal in Scranton. Every time he remembered it, he felt irritated by the old woman's arrogance and regretted that he hadn't been more adept in his arguments. After weeks passed with no further word from her or Monica, it seemed that the final burial plot would indeed be earned "the old-fashioned way" (as Archie put it).

Greg's cell phone chirped one Friday evening as he settled into his recliner after a relentless week.

"Hi, Doc. It's Archie Early."

"Hey, Arch. What's up?"

"I just thought you should know. I'm over here at the county hospital."

"Everything all right?"

Archie sounded distracted, and Greg recognized the distinct clatter of a hospital lobby in the background.

"They brought her here. In an ambulance. I followed them in my car. I just thought you should know."

"Who do you mean?"

"Doc, it's Starlight. She's in the ER right now."

Within five minutes Greg was racing northward out of Emmitsville toward the hospital. He figured if he pushed the speed limit he could cover the distance in about twenty minutes.

Fragments from his conversation with Archie cycled through his mind. "She just slumped forward in the car . . . someone did CPR until the ambulance arrived . . . she was out cold when they took her away."

The glass doors to the ER slid open so slowly that Greg squeezed through the gap sideways. He saw Archie sitting in the nearly empty waiting area.

"How's she doing?"

Archie's face was pale. The wrinkles under his eyes and on his forehead seemed to droop under an invisible weight.

"I haven't heard anything."

"You OK?"

"I don't know, Doc. We spent the day together. Went out for a picnic. She fell asleep on the ride home. I'd just pulled into a gas station when she slumped over. Hit her head on the dash. You think maybe I braked too hard? It didn't seem like it, but maybe—"

"I'm guessing you had nothing to do with it, Archie. Let me see what I can find out."

Greg approached the registration desk and explained that Starlight was his patient. He waited until a man in light-blue scrubs emerged from the wooden doors near the desk.

"Dr. Patterson?"

Greg raised his hand. "That's me."

"I'm Jeremy Harris—on call tonight. I understand that Mrs. Goodwell is your patient?"

"Yes, sir. I've heard your name before, but I don't think our paths have ever crossed."

"Yes, same for me. I'm glad you came in. I have a few questions for you about Mrs. Goodwell. Are you able to follow me back to a conference room where we can chat?"

"Yes. Absolutely."

Dr. Harris led him into a small room just inside the double doors.

"So, you're her primary?"

"Yes."

"Can you give me any highlights I should know?"

"She had a rough bout of pneumonia a while back, and she deals with near-constant pain in her right hip from a fracture. It keeps her off her feet a decent amount of the time."

"That's it?"

"That's all I can recall, yes."

Dr. Harris pursed his lips. "That is unfortunate. I was hoping you could confirm a CAVC diagnosis."

"CAVC?" Greg racked his brain to recall the meaning of the acronym. He hadn't encountered it much since his days in medical school. "No, I've never picked up on that at all."

"No heart murmur?" Greg shook his head. "From what I've seen on the echo, I feel almost certain it's CAVC. The scars on her chest indicate some sort of heart surgery in the past. My guess is that she had it repaired as a child but the work hasn't held up. Deterioration of the patches may have come on recently."

Greg felt his face redden. "I'm not sure how I could've missed something like that. For eight years?" He didn't mention that for nearly half of those years he'd seen Starlight in her kitchen or living room much more often than his office.

The room suddenly felt cramped and stuffy. Greg wondered what Dr. Harris thought of him and the obvious oversight he'd made with his patient.

"To be frank, a confirmed diagnosis may be a moot point by now. She's not well." Greg ran his fingers through his hair and let out a slow exhale. Dr. Harris continued, "If you'd like, I can take you in."

Greg nodded.

When he returned to the waiting area twenty minutes later, he found Archie sitting in the same chair.

"What's the word, Doc?"

Greg snapped into physician mode—twenty-five years of training and experience overriding emotion. "Archie, I'm afraid I've got bad news about Starlight. It's possible she won't be alive much longer. Her brain activity is minimal, and the doctors are doing all they can to keep her with us."

The news seemed to hit Archie slowly. After several seconds, he said, "Jeez. Just like that."

"I'm—sorry." Greg's voice broke slightly.

Archie turned toward the exit. "I have to go. Are you sticking around here?"

"Uh—yes. I plan on staying through the night if I need to. Are you OK?"

"I guess so. I just hope it wasn't my fault. Braking too hard or something like that."

"Archie." Greg moved a step closer and looked up into the older man's eyes. "You had nothing to do with this. The ER doctor believes—and I think he's correct—that she has a congenital heart defect. A heart issue she was born with. It's called CAVC."

"I had no idea."

"I didn't either. She never mentioned it." The sting of the missed diagnosis was still fresh. "If this is true, then it wouldn't have mattered who she was with or what she was doing at the time. It's likely that her heart has been failing for a while. You understand what I mean?"

Archie nodded. "All these years walking around with her heart broken."

"Something like that."

"Like I said, I'm gonna scoot. I'll probably come back later and look for you, OK?"

"Sure thing."

Archie walked out, leaving Greg in a waiting area that was quiet and calm for the moment. The few people there were either dozing, reading, or scrolling.

Greg exited into a corridor, wandering until he came to a wing of the hospital opposite the ER. This section of the building housed a walk-in clinic and several specialized departments that were closed for the weekend. In a dimly lit alcove, he pulled one chair around to face another. Propping his feet up on the second chair, he nestled down in his makeshift couch and closed his eyes.

But he was unable to doze off. Instead, he remembered a conversation that had taken place in Starlight's living room a few weeks earlier.

Starlight had been asking about his mother—what he remembered of her and of his family's tumultuous days between her death and her funeral.

"Do you think you'll see her again?"

"My mom?"

"Sure. Don't you believe in the afterlife? Heaven, hell, and everything in between?"

"I grew up with all that. I used to feel strongly about it, but not so much these last few years."

"Why?"

"Not sure exactly. It's all just conjecture anyway. A high-stakes guessing game. In my experience, everyone loses their swagger when the end is barreling down on them."

"Well, of course they do."

"What do you mean?"

"It's part of the process, Greg."

"What process?"

"Faith. Belief. Religion. It's not a static condition. It's a process. Most everyone goes through at least four or five stages along the way."

"You're talking like some sort of expert in the field."

"Not really. I'm just a Methodist—born and baptized."

"I never knew that!"

"Oh, yeah. I even earned a couple of perfect attendance awards for Sunday school when I was a kid."

"So these stages of religion. You've been through them?"

"Of course. Conversion (nine years old). Zeal (most of my teenage years). The confusion stage really hit hard in my early twenties. I was turned all inside out."

In the weeks since Greg had made his unsuccessful bid for romance, their friendship had deepened and stretched, and Starlight had told him much more about herself. Growing up in Kansas, leaving home at sixteen years old, a three-month marriage at age twenty . . . a stillborn baby girl. Though she shared many details, Greg suspicioned that she left out parts of her story.

"How'd you get past it?"

"I didn't at first. My confusion morphed into disillusionment. Big-time. I was guarded and cynical—kind of like you."

"Ouch!"

"Just being honest. Took me about a decade to get to the last stage."

"How do you know it's the last one?"

"I just know."

"So tell me, oh wise one, what is this stage of peace and tranquility you've reached?"

"Compromise."

"Sounds sketchy. Most religions frown on compromise."

"Not compromising *in* your religion. I mean compromising *with* your religion. There's no system of belief out there that will perfectly answer every question and completely fill every hole, so to speak. Everyone's gonna face their own disillusionment at some point. The only way I know of to get out of that is to own up to the questions—answer the ones you can and live with the ones you can't. Compromise."

He'd never been good at that.

He gave up trying to sleep around midnight. He returned the chairs to their original positions and trudged back to the ER.

"Dr. Patterson?" It was the woman at the registration desk. "I was about to call you. Your patient, Mrs. Goodwell, passed away a few minutes ago. Dr. Harris said you're free to go back into the room and see her, if you'd like."

Greg found her room and closed the door behind him.

The nurses had already removed the tubes from her nose and mouth and the IVs from her arms. She was on her back, arms at her sides under the bedsheet and eyes closed. Her hair looked as though a nurse had pulled it away from her cheeks and tucked it behind her head.

Greg stared as if he could pierce through the layers of skin and bone on her chest to see straight to her heart and the fatal defect between its chambers. She'd been born with it and lived with it every day: a hole in the tissue undermining her heart's attempts to function, pulling her toward disaster. In many ways, the last fifty years of her life had been a gift.

"Or a cruel joke," Greg muttered.

He stood at the foot of the bed and allowed the thoughts that had been dogging him for the last hour to rush through his head.

In all his life he'd only felt truly seen and known by two people. Two women.

"Well . . . three, I guess."

With Starlight's passing that night, all of them were gone. Separated from him by death or by distance.

He wouldn't speak to her; he'd never understood why anyone did, in such situations. He wouldn't cry. It wasn't that he didn't want to, but tears rarely came to him. He moved to the left side of the bed, leaned forward, and touched her forehead with two fingers. Her skin was still warm, but felt clammy and stiff.

He turned out the light as he left the room.

CHAPTER 20

*G*reg sat in the small room adjacent to the Hunt Chapel reserved for families of the deceased. Everything around him was soft. The carpet was thick and plush, the couches so stuffed that he felt enveloped in upholstery. The lighting was dim and the air was cool. Each detail seemed designed to lighten the burden of grief carried in by those who entered.

This was the first time Greg had ever been in it.

There was a quiet knock, and the door swung open wide enough for Ambrose to poke his head in. "It's ten minutes till we start. Can I get you anything?"

Greg pointed toward a small refrigerator in the corner. "Nah. I already grabbed a bottle of water. Thanks."

"Absolutely. I'll come get you just before one o'clock."

"Have you seen Opal out there?"

"No sign of her yet."

While Greg had often witnessed the Wannamakers operating in their roles as funeral-home directors, he'd never before been the recipient of their services. He was impressed by their professionalism and sincerity. They'd helped and encouraged him through a week that had been far more difficult than he had expected.

During the previous seven days he'd had to negotiate his feelings about Starlight's death and stave off questions from Gladys and other curious townspeople. He had also discovered that he was responsible for the funeral arrangements—a surprise delivered to him by Archie Early arriving at the office with a manila envelope. Inside were Starlight's will, naming Greg as executor, and an undated letter.

Archie offered little in the way of explanation. "She asked me a while back to give it to you if the need ever arose."

According to the clock on the wall, Greg had eight minutes left. He slid his cell phone from his suit pocket, pulled up his contact list, and tapped the name at the top.

"Hello?"

He marveled at how mature her voice sounded. A lot like her mother.

"Hey, kiddo."

"Dad!" Summer called out with delight. "How are you?"

"I'm OK."

"Not sure I believe that. You sound a little grumpy!"

"Actually, I wanted to ask you a question."

"What's up?"

"Remember walking in the cemetery last fall? You said that a lot of what people do in terms of funerals and last wishes is a way of making themselves feel better when their time comes."

"I remember."

"My question is—do you believe it makes a difference? I'm not trying to debate it. I genuinely want to know if you think that's true."

She didn't answer right away. "Yes. I really do. I think we all find ways to cope."

"With oblivion."

"There's probably a better way to say it, but yes. That's the gist. Why are you bringing it up now?"

A lump formed in Greg's throat. "Do you remember the woman we met on our bike ride?"

"Starlight. Sure!"

"She died last Friday night."

"Oh my gosh! Dad! I'm so sorry." She paused to grapple with the news. "Was it expected?"

"Not for me."

"Oh, Dad!" Her voice strained as if she might start to cry. "What awful news. I'm sure that hits you hard. Are you OK?"

"I think so. Actually, I'm at the funeral home right now. The service is beginning in a few minutes. She wanted me to lead it."

"Oh no!"

"What?"

"Well, I know how much you hate stuff like that."

"I'll be fine. She didn't have anything elaborate planned. It won't take long."

"I wish I could be there. To support you and celebrate Starlight's life."

"You only met her once. You don't know much about her life."

"I know she lived one. That alone is a pretty remarkable thing."

He leaned his head back into the cushion and let out a long, low sigh.

"Yes. You're right." He consulted the clock. "It's almost one. I better get out there. I love you."

"I love you too, Dad. I hope everything goes well for you."

Greg walked through the side door of the chapel and approached the podium. In front of him was the burnished blue casket with silver trim he'd chosen earlier that week. He surveyed the audience briefly. The room was less than half full—around 150 in attendance, and he couldn't help wondering how many came merely out of curiosity. He saw

Archie several rows back on the left side, but as far as Greg could tell, Opal was not in the room.

"Good afternoon. Thank you all for being here. I've been asked to lead today's memorial service for Starlight Goodwell.

"Starlight didn't put together a detailed plan for her funeral. I imagine that's because she wasn't expecting to have one quite so soon." He said this to quell speculation that she'd known her time was close and that the final Cotterman plot would be hers. More than a few around town—including Gladys—had suggested as much. Though Greg always denied the allegation, he'd secretly thought the same thing several times.

"And I've been unable to locate any next of kin to get their input. She did leave a letter with instructions to read it to you today." He looked down at her handwritten words on the papers he held. Most of the letter was meant for him only. The portion to be read in public was just a few lines long. He dropped the sheets onto the podium and took a tiny step back from the microphone.

"Before I do that, I'd like to say a few words in her honor." Once he'd announced this, a stroke of panic gripped him. He hadn't planned on giving a speech and didn't know what to say next.

"I was honored to be Starlight's doctor for nearly a decade. She and Everett were great patients. Constantly kind to me and receptive to advice. It's always difficult to lose a patient, no matter who they are, and that was certainly true with both of them.

"But Starlight was more than just a patient to me. She was my friend. She didn't have many of those in town, and we clicked with each other in a way that was really special. She was funny, smart, and unpredictable. I'll never forget the impact her friendship made on me.

"But over the last week, I've had to wrestle with an uncomfortable thought that keeps circling around and around in my brain. As much as I cared about her as a patient and a friend, there's a lot about her I never had the chance to find out.

"I know she lived in Kansas as a kid. She grew up going to a Methodist church each Sunday with her sister. She spent most of her life out in the Midwest working all sorts of jobs until she came here to Emmitsville ten years ago.

"That's basically all I know. Like I said a minute ago, I wasn't even able to locate any of her family. In the days since she passed away, I've come to realize that there are large chunks of her story I'll never get to hear. Now, is that because I didn't think to ask, or because she didn't think to tell me? Probably a little of both.

"I'm not saying all of this to get you to feel badly for me. My point is—I guess my point is that every life we encounter is a remarkable thing. Everyone's story deserves our respect. And I think it's important that we try to hear and learn each other's stories as best we can."

He looked back down at the letter and skimmed the words he was about to read. He cleared his throat before continuing.

"You never know. They might surprise you in the end.

"Here's the letter she wanted me to share with you: 'I, Linda "Starlight" Goodwell, being of sound mind and body (or as near to that as I can tell) do hereby request that the following actions be taken in my honor once I am deceased. First, that my estate be distributed to the charities and individuals listed in my will. Second, that my body be cremated and my ashes turned over to Mr. Archibald Early to be stored or spread in a manner and place of his choosing. Third, that my casket be donated to someone who died young and unexpectedly. Fourth, if the timing of my death is such that I am to be the recipient of the final burial plot in Cotterman Cemetery and Memorial Gardens, that ownership of the plot be officially transferred from me to Miss Opal Ridgley. Paid in full. Irrevocable. Nontransferable and all that other legal language that makes it rock solid. These are my final wishes.'"

As eyebrows and whispered exclamations rose around the room, he wished he'd planned more for the service: A song. Another eulogy. A picture montage. He was gripped by the moment and wanted every person in the room to see and know Starlight the way he did.

Instead, he concluded the service and retreated to the family waiting room. Ambrose followed, loosening his tie as he sat on the couch.

"I thought what you said about her was very good."

Greg had already removed his tie. "Thanks. What's the word out there?"

"I didn't overhear much. People are surprised, of course. But no one really seemed to be questioning Starlight's right to give the last plot away. As far as I'm concerned it now belongs to Opal. We'll have it ready for her when she needs it."

"And then . . .?"

Ambrose looked through the doorway into the Hunt Chapel. "And that will be the end of that, I suppose."

Two weeks later, Greg stood in the corner of Archie Early's sprawling backyard.

"She never mentioned any particular place," Archie explained, "so I decided to go with a flower garden out here. Course it's not much to look at now. It will be beautiful in the spring when everything is blooming."

The empty garden plot was covered with fresh bark mulch and edged with oblong paving stones. In the center was a small, simple headstone with one word engraved on it.

"It's perfect," said Greg.

Archie stepped back. "Anyway, I'll leave you be for now. You're welcome to come out anytime you want and spend a few moments with her."

"Can I ask you a question?"

"Sure."

"Do you know why she did it? All of it—the letter, the funeral, Opal, me?"

"I've asked myself that same thing. Ever since she first told me what she was cooking up."

"Wait, you knew about it? Since when?"

"When she gave me the envelope and told me what she had in mind."

Greg remembered how close he'd come to ignoring Starlight's last wishes and letting her have the final Cotterman plot instead of Opal. He hadn't even considered that Archie might know what was coming. "You were OK with it?"

"It's not like there was a good chance she'd actually get to work her plan. And when it did happen—what was I gonna say? Too late to talk her out of it, you know?"

"Yeah."

Archie grinned and nodded at the headstone. "Even then, I was OK with it. Opal is who she is, and Starlight—well, I suspect you know better than me that she was tough to fit in a box."

"Yup."

"So I figure it all shook out the way it was supposed to." He turned toward the house. "Like I said, you're welcome any time. Shoot! Maybe one day we can pop over to the Blue Dot and grab coffee. Swap some Starlight stories?"

"I'd like that. Thanks."

Alone in front of the garden, Greg folded his hands behind his back. It was early evening, but already dusk was overtaking the valley. Autumn was hardening into winter once again. He had to strain his eyes to see the letters engraved in the granite slab as they faded into darkness:

STARLIGHT

CHAPTER 21

$\mathcal{I}$n the cemetery on the northwest side of Denver, Greg stood ankle-deep in a drift of snow. It was early November, and the first winter storm of the season had rushed through a day earlier. On the other side of the large stone slab, Sandy, Alicia, and Summer huddled together.

"Thank you all for being willing to do this."

"Wouldn't have missed it for the world!" said Sandy enthusiastically.

Greg could feel the redness tinting his cheeks—whether from cold or regret, he didn't know.

"The truth is, we should've all been here together last year. I messed that up. I'm sorry."

Summer smiled. "We love you, Dad."

Greg pulled a couple sheets of paper from the inner pocket of his coat. "It's cold out here, so I'll try to keep this short. I thought a verse reading would be appropriate."

Sandy was already crying. "That's sounds wonderful. Very special. Dad would love it."

Greg unfolded the papers as he spoke. "I was flipping through his old Bible last night, and I saw that he had this passage underlined. To be fair, he had a lot of passages underlined, but—this one sorta resonated with me, so I printed off the words. I didn't want to bring the Bible out here and ruin it. So . . . here it is. It's from Psalm 71: 'In thee, O Lord, do I put my trust. Let me never be put to confusion. Be thou my strong habitation, whereunto I may continually resort. For thou art my hope, O Lord God. Thou art my trust from my youth. Cast me not off in the time of old age. Forsake me not when my strength faileth.'"

Greg let the words linger before he continued.

"The other thing I wanted to do was read Dad's obituary. This should have gone out last year, but . . . I never submitted it. Again, I'm sorry."

The wind picked up and he fought to keep his voice steady against the rush of cold air.

"'On Tuesday, this world became a little less compassionate than it was the day before because Larry Patterson died unexpectedly that morning. Larry's friends and family know that he was one of the kindest, gentlest souls around. From his childhood years in Pueblo, Colorado, as the only child of George and Rita Patterson to his adulthood as the husband of Korrine (deceased), father of Sandy and Greg, and teacher of countless junior-high music students at Walker Middle School, Larry Patterson's life was filled with acts of compassion, empathy, generosity, and care for his fellow human beings. He faithfully communicated his love of music to generations of students. He bravely persevered in raising two children as a widower. He treated friends like family, and family like best friends. His unexpected departure leaves a void that is keenly felt by many. It is the desire of those closest to him that his legacy of generosity and human decency is carried on in the lives of those who knew him.'"

"It's perfect, Dad." Summer sniffled.

"Just beautiful," said Sandy.

Greg refolded the papers and placed them in his pocket. "Well, I say we get out of this cold air and warm up!"

Summer and Sandy walked arm in arm toward the car, parked on the road edging the cemetery. Greg and Alicia followed. At the last row of graves, Alicia put her hand on Greg's arm, and they stopped.

"I'm really proud of you for doing this today," Alicia said, looking at him with her direct gaze. "For getting us together. I think it was really important for all of us."

"It was pretty short—"

"It was good, Greg. Very special. Thank you." She put her hand on his arm again.

"Oh, you know me!" He tried to sound lighthearted.

"Yes. I do. That's why it means so much."

He didn't know what to say.

"I've been thinking the last few days that I'd like to sit down with you. I'd like us to talk. I feel like there's some things we should say."

His throat tightened. "Yeah. I think that would be good."

They hurried to join Sandy and Summer in the warmth of the waiting car.

Returning to Emmitsville, Greg was soon engrained in most of his old routines—familiar and comforting. Ambrose and Allen focused on their roles as cemetery custodians now that they had just one burial left to perform.

It didn't take place for a full two and a half years.

Opal Ridgley died under hospice care in her own home after an extended illness. At her request, there was no funeral or memorial service. Ambrose and Allen lowered her coffin into the final spot in Cotterman three days after she passed away. They installed her headstone the following day.

Greg took an extra-long lunch break and walked from his office to Opal's final resting place.

The headstone read simply:

Opal Ridgley
1935–2021

Several times since Starlight's death, he'd tried to arrange a visit with Opal. He was hoping to see in her what Starlight had seen. Despite a number of prevailing theories, no one in town knew for sure why Starlight had given away her spot. She took her secret with her.

But Opal wouldn't return Greg's calls, and she'd switched to a different medical practice a few months after Starlight's funeral. He thought about driving out to her house, but didn't follow through on it. They never spoke again after their confrontation in the office building in Scranton.

He was alone in the cemetery, and he whispered the words. "No hard feelings, OK?"

It was a clear, sunny sky over Emmitsville. Greg took his time walking back to the office. He knew Gladys would be annoyed that he'd been gone so long and was running late for his next appointment. Still, he paused on the sidewalk to read the sign above his front door.

Dr. Gregory Patterson, M.D.
General Practice

When he'd first moved to town, he'd considered various names for his practice. In recent years a trend had emerged toward corporate-sounding names like *Wellspring Health* or *Valley Medical*. He stuck with his own name because nothing else seemed to click.

Now he smiled at his sign. The name worked nicely. *His* name. It was simple and straightforward. He liked things that way. It was his practice—his place.

And Emmitsville was his home.

ACKNOWLEDGMENTS

I want to thank Lee Ann at Illuminations Editing for several years of honest, incisive, yet encouraging feedback. I've learned a great deal from her in this process, and she helped me to keep believing that the story is worth telling. I must also mention those who read the early drafts and asked such helpful questions. You all were great test subjects for this story. Thanks to Stephanie for giving it a final polish and to Jenneth for exceeding my expectations with her cover artwork. A very special thanks to all those who donated to the "big check" surprise and in turn invested in me at a moment when it looked like the project might be dead for good.

My three children have tolerated my work on this project for a long time. Thanks guys! My wife has been unwavering in her conviction that I not only *could* write a book but also that I *would*. I'm forever grateful to her for blazing a trail for our family.

ALSO BY ANDREW D. DOAN

Plays

The Elixir of Love

The McMillan Way

Short Fiction

Intruders

Crouching in the Corner of Her Eye

The Last Sunday in September

The Becker Test

Podcasts

This Is by Andrew D. Doan

All of these titles are available at andrewddoan.com

CPSIA information can be obtained
at www.ICGtesting.com
Printed in the USA
BVHW070228310821
615478BV00002B/9

9 781737 561002